Only God Can Judge Me

Written by Ms. Lolita D. Newman

ISBN-13: 978-0692532379
ISBN-10: 0692532374

Cover Art: AMB Branding

Published By Kenerly Presents

Charlotte North Carolina

Chapter One

Cold fall morning. Sun was shining but it wasn't doing much. As the gates opened, Lee stepped out. Lee was 5ft. 200 lbs. Lee was caramel complexion with hazel eyes. Her hair, in braids, was a two tone color of light and dark brown. Lee was wearing hiking boots with a white tee underneath a grey hoodie. She had on a black Nike hat turned backwards. Adjusting her glasses, Lee stepped into the parking lot, took a deep breath and lit a cigarette. Taking a puff, Lee begun to scan the parking lot. Finally seeing what she was looking for, she grinned taking another puff and puts the cigarette out.

Lee picked up her black duffle bag and headed over to a 2000 Blue 4 door Chevy Tahoe. Getting out was Lisa, her girlfriend. Lisa was light skin.5'5 and weighed 195lbs. She had straight dark hair that came down to her mid back. Lisa father was black, her mom, Cherokee Indian. Lisa walked up to Lee and hugged her, kissing her on the cheek. Both headed back to the car. Lee put her duffle bag in the back seat and slid into the passenger seat as Lisa got in and begun to drive home.

Lee lit up another cigarette and leaned back into the seat. *A-Con's Lockup* was playing on the radio but Lee paid it no attention. Her mind drifted back to her two year stay for probation violation for drug trafficking among her many offenses. Lee had problems with the law before; drug sales, armed robbery, assault with a deadly weapon and CCW. Inside, Lee got her GED and went to counseling. Her probation officer went to bat for her and got her time reduced from having to serve until she would be twenty-one. It was also at this time, that Lee got emancipation and became a legal adult. She also agreed to continue counseling and to find a job.

Lee turned and looked at Lisa and smiled. *"She had been with me through out all this,"* thinking to herself.

Grabbing Lisa hand, Lee gently squeezed them and said *"thank you."*

　　"What's that for?" Lisa asked.
　　"Just for being there," Lee answered.
　　"That's what friends do."
　　"Yeah," she add taking a puff of her cigarette, *"But I know it's been hard, I mean having to put with my bullshit. I wanted you to know how much I appreciate you being there."*

　　Lisa smiled at Lee and leaned in to kiss her. Lee laid her head back against the headrest and continued to allow her mind to wonder. Lee lost her father three years ago at the age of fourteen to kidney failure from diabetes. Her and her step mom never got along; she blamed Lee for her problems with her marriage to Lee dad. When her dad died, Lee stepped mom put her out and Lee had to hustle just to survive.

　　Then she met Lisa and moved in with her. At first there were some rough moments. Lisa being older, tried to be a mother to Lee, always correcting her or chadtising her for things she did; like coming home late, or how she dressed or who she hung out with. Lee didn't want another "mom," what she wanted was a friend, someone to talk to, someone to love and who loved her unconditionally. After awhile, Lisa became that. Lisa understood that a mother figure was not what Lee needed.

　　The age was not the only problem they had to endure. It was Lisa occupation. Lee had met Lisa through a mutual friend who took her to a nightclub where Lisa danced. Lisa 5'5 body frame was flawless, considering she had a son. Her caramel Indian complexion with her long dark hair made Lisa irresistible. Lisa had her name tattooed on her neck with her tribal sign on her lower back. She also had a tattoo of a red rose on her left ankle. On her right bicep was her mother's name enclave in a half moon. This wasn't what attractive Lee to Lisa though, it was her eyes. Lisa eyes were a soft, loving grey

4

color. She would always tell Lisa, *"When I look into your eyes, I know everything will be alright. They never lie."*

Later that night, Lee and Lisa struck up a conversation with each other and Lisa asked Lee to move in. Since Lee stepmom could have cared less about her, Lee said yes and moved in that night. Lee didn't have much, just a few things. Lisa pretty much took care of Lee, buying her clothes and providing for her needs. Lisa understood the satuation Lee was in and didn't mind doing the things she did. She would tell her all the time, *"I do these things not because I have too but because I love you."*

Sometimes though Lisa had to remind her that just because she loved her, her love was not to be taken for granted, don't assume anything. A few times, Lee found out the hard way how true that was. One night Lee was out with Kelly, her friend and arrived home late, drunk and showing out. They got into a heated argument and Lee got mad and threw a glass at her, missing her. Lisa pissed, tried to put Lee out. At that moment, Lee got mad and put her hands on Lisa, striking her in the face. Realizing what she did, Lee immediately started to apologize. Lisa quietly walked into the bedroom, got her gun and walked back into the living room and pointed at Lee. *"If you value your life, you need to leave now,"* Lisa said softly. Lee left. It took 3 weeks before Lisa let Lee come back and another month before she truly trusted her. Lisa told her the next time would be her last and Lee believed her.

Many people said their relationship would not last with the age gap but through it all, they manage to stay together. They learned and relearned how to trust, be open and not lie to one another. Most important though, they loved each other unconditionally.

"Kelly will be over later with Alexis." Lisa turned to said to Lee.

"Cool, I haven't seen her in a minute," Lee smiled.

"Are you surprise?" If it wasn't for her, your ass wouldn't have been lockup."* Lisa irritated by Lee's reaction.

"Don't start please. I know you don't care for her."

"Sheez, don't care is an understatement. Babe, she's rude and inconsiderate. Look how she treats Alexis. She cheats on her, hitting her, calling her all kind of bitches and sluts."

"Lex is no angel though; she starts shit too and creeps on Kelly too."

Lisa pulled into the driveway, parked the car and turned it off. Lisa grabbed the wheel with both hands and sighed before looking at Lee.

"Both of them got issues, I agree but it what you did for Kelly that got you put in juvenile." Lisa grabbed Lee's braids and gently pulled on them. *"I love you and I'm happy your home. I miss you."*

"I miss you too," smiled at Lisa.

"Then please promise me that you'll be careful when you and Kelly are together."

"You know I can't make that promise," Lee said looking down at the floorboard.

"If you truly love me, you will."

"You know I do," laughing, *"I'll try."* Lee leaned over and kissed Lisa.

Getting out the car, Lee reached in the backseat and grabbed her duffle bag. As Lisa headed into the house, Lee stood in the yard and looked up at the house, she chuckled to herself; *"Damn it felt good to be home,"* she said under her breath as she headed inside.

Chapter Two

The house was a one floor plan with a basement. On the outside, the house was blue with white trimming and a little flowerbed. A wind chime hung beginning to sway back and forth as the wind blew. On the front porch was two blue and white wicker chairs with a matching table and a swing between them.

Inside the house was a beige couch against the north wall with a matching chair, love seat, recliner and Ottawa. A black coffee table with magazines sat in the middle of the room with matching end tables and lamps on either side. Across from the sofa was a mantel with pictures, candles and awards along it. Along the walls were Thomas Kincaid paintings of outdoors and cabins and paintings of different Indians tribes, including one with Lisa ancestors. A painting of Christ with his arms opened and angels around him was also hanging on the wall.

Putting down her duffle bag, Lee went into the kitchen where Lisa was fixing a sandwich. After washing her hands and drying them off, Lee sat down at the table as Lisa came over and sat the plate and a glass of juice down in front of her. Lisa sat down next to her.

"Your caseworker called this morning before I left to pick you up."

Taking a bite of her sandwich, Lee chewed then took a sip of juice. Wiping her mouth, Lee reclined back in the chair.

"What she want?"
"She said, she got hold of your sister and wants to come by and talk to you about it."
"So when she supposes to be coming by?"
"Sometime today, why?"

Finishing her sandwich and juice, Lee got up and went to the sink and washed her plate and glass. When she was done, Lee grabbed a towel, dried her hands and went back to the table and sat down.

"Since I got home, I was hoping to hang out with Kelly since she was coming over."

Lisa annoyed, "So you rather hang out with Kelly then with your girl?"

Laughing, Lee leaned in and playful bites Lisa on the neck. Lisa frustrated pushed Lee away, got up from the table and walked into the bedroom and closed the door behind her. Lee followed her but when she tried to open the door, it's locked. Lee knocked on the door but got no response. After a few minutes, Lee heard movement in the room and then heard the click as the door was unlocked.

Stepping into the room, Lee saw Lisa lying in bed with her back towards her. *Ebony Eyes* was playing on the radio.

"I love you...oh baby...
Ebony eyes....
I need you...and I betcha didn't know that...
Ebony eyes..."

Climbing into the bed, Lee held Lisa in her arms. Gently, Lee begun kissing Lisa's neck softly while stroking her hair. Finally, Lisa turned over and faced her. Lee saw Lisa had been crying. Lee wiped away the tears. Pulling her closer, Lee held her, whispering, "Everything will be fine."

"I love you... (Girl)...
Betcha didn't know that...
Ebony eyes..."

Lisa got up and went into the bathroom to clean her face. She came back into the bedroom and sat on the edge of the bed. Lee sat next to her.

"There's nothing more than I want to do then spend time with you, you know that."

Lisa tried to maintain control, *"but every time Kelly came around, it's always drama. I'm tired of it and you should be too."*

"But she is coming over, what I'm supposed to do? Besides that's how Kelly is."

"Why do you always defended her?" Lisa became irritated.

Lee leaned back on the bed kicking her feet together, *"she really doesn't have anybody, except me and Alexis."*

Sarcastically, *"I wonder why."* Stretch out next to Lee with her head in Lee's arms.

"Besides, she always had been there for me."

"Lee, all I'm saiding is Kelly is nothing but trouble. Look at this last time around, for God sake, you ended up in juvenile because of her. Baby, next time..." Lisa voice trailed off.

"I know your concern but everything will be ok, I promise. I'm home now, with you. Can we please try to enjoy the moment?"

Lisa frustrated at Lee, got up. As Lee went to grab her, Lisa pulled away. Lee jumped up.

Standing face to face with Lisa, Lee started to feel the rage and emotions build up inside. Lisa did not back down instead stepping to her.

"So you think you hard now? What, you want to hit me again!" I yield, *"I already warned you!"*

Lee didn't said anything instead just looked at Lisa.

"She doesn't give a damn about herself or anyone else!" Lisa voice rose. *"Why can't you see that, all she does is uses people, taking them down with her!"*

Lee threw open the bedroom door and walked out, Lisa was behind her. Lisa reached out for Lee arm but Lee jerked away. Sitting in the recliner, Lee put her hands behind her head and stared into space. This was not the homecoming Lee was looking forward to. All she wanted was to kick it with her friends, be with her girl and chill. Not this bullshit.

Lisa went over to Lee and reached out for her hand but pulled back when Lee looked at her. Lisa took a seat on the loveseat.

"Baby," Lisa softly. *"Kelly's going to get you killed. I know she's your friend but at some point, loyalty stops when it became too much. I know you feel like you owe her but not your life and not my life with you."*

Lee still said nothing, looking up at the ceiling, trying to calm down. Lisa saw she wasn't going to respond. She threw her hands in the air in defeat and went back to the bedroom.

Lee continued to sat there, staring at the wall, hands behind her head. Lee understood why Lisa did not like Kelly, she got that and Lisa right. Every time something went down, Kelly always somewhere in the middle, pulling Lee right into it. It was Kelly's car she was in, Kelly's drugs, not Lee's. What was she suppose to do? Kelly told her that the court wouldn't do anything to her because of her age. Lee couldn't bail.

Kelly already had two strikes against her and being caught with 2kg. of cocaine would have put her away for a long time. *"Your only fifteen, the most they would give you is six months, maybe a year,"* Kelly said. So Lee went along with it and pleaded guilty to the drugs and the hidden .45 (Lee didn't know about the gun until the cops found it and showed her). The judge didn't care though about Lee's age. She was already on probation for truant from school, a runaway, curfew violation, assault and weed procession. He was going to make an example of her so he sentence Lee to juvenile until she turned twenty-one.

The first few days were difficult. Lee was in fights everyday with other girls, provoked by the guards and almost raped by one of the girls. Lee spent most of her time in isolation trying to keep it together. After a few months, she was allowed to have visators and Lisa would come often. Lee believed that if it wasn't for Lisa visat, she wouldn't have made it. Lisa encouraged Lee to stay strong and convinced her to get her GED. Lee even got the much needed counseling inside to help her deal with her emotions.

Along with Lisa and the counselor recommendation, the judge allowed Lee to serve only two years of her sentence for good behavior. One condition, Lee was put on back on probation until she turned twenty-one, continue counseling and find a job. Lisa also wanted Lee to stay away from Kelly. She felt Kelly was a bad influence. Maybe Lisa was right but Lee couldn't abandon her friend. Kelly was there for her when her dad died and her stepmom put her out. When Lee came out about her lifestyle and people started acting funny, Kelly would said, *"People are jealous and assholes. Be yourself."* When people tried to hurt her, Kelly would defend her. There were plenty of moments when Lee and Kelly had to square up because people would act funny or said something stupid. One time in particular, Kelly found out that three girls from school were planning to jump Lee when she got to school that morning. Instead of telling Lee, Kelly went to the ring leader and confronted her. By the time it was over, Kelly had slammed the girl into the lockers. That year, no one said anything else to Lee about her lifestyle.

Lee finally got up and went into the bedroom where Lisa was. She went over to the bed, leaned in and hugged Lisa, saiding, *"I'm sorry."* Lisa looked at her and smiled. She grabbed Lee and pulled her into the bed with her. As Lee lied next to her, she looked into Lisa's eyes.

"You know what first attractive me to you?"
Lisa laughed, *"What?"*
"Your eyes, when I look deep inside, they show me your beauty deep within."
Lisa blushed, *"Go on."*
"You mean a lot to me, I don't want to lose you. You're my best friend, I love you."
"I love you too," Lisa stroked Lee's face, *"but baby, I just feel..."*
Lee placed her fingers to Lisa lips, *"shush, right now all I want to do is lay here and enjoy you."*

Lee gently kissed Lisa on her lips then on her ears, moving down her neck. Lisa reacted with every touch as Lee pulled her closer. Lee laid in bed, holding Lisa, remembering all the good times they had and promising herself never to leave Lisa alone again.

Chapter Three

A knock at the door brings Lisa out the room. At the door was a middle age white woman. The woman introduced herself as Mrs. Gladys Carlton, the court appointed caseworker. Mrs. Carlton at 47 is 4'5 and is a round, plump built. She had brunette hair mix with slight gray and wore wide rim glasses.

Lisa let her in and had her take a seat in the recliner chair. Lisa excused herself as Mrs. Carlton took off her coat and went into the bedroom to get Lee. A few minutes later, Lee and Lisa came into the living room and joined Mrs. Carlton, taking a seat on the sofa.

Mrs. Carlton took out of her briefcase some papers and hands them to Lee. The papers were conditions of Lee's early release. The requirements and the consequences if there not followed. Lee looked over the papers, nodded in agreement and sign them.

Lee got up and gave Mrs. Carlton back the papers and sat back down on the sofa rubbing her hands back and forth across her sweat pants. Lisa saw Lee was nervous. She gently squeezed her hand and let her know it was ok. Lee relaxed. Mrs. Carlton put the papers back into the briefcase and crossed her legs. A few moments passed before she spoke.

"As you know, we located you sister and have been in touch with her about you. She would like to meet you."

Mrs. Carlton handed Lee a picture of her sister.

"Her name is Renee Wilson. She is thirty-one and had a little boy."

Lee looked at the picture and passed it to Lisa.

"So why she wants to see me after all these years?" Lee *said* curiously.

"Well, you were only a baby when your mom died, Renee was fourteen. When your father came and took you to raise you that was the last time Renee seen you."

"But I don't know her or anything about my mom, well except for what little my dad told me."

"That's why she wants to see you. Before your mom died, she told Renee who your father was and how to reach him and you. But because of legality, Renee was unable to locate you, until now."

"Why now?" Lee still not convinced.

Reaching back into her briefcase, Mrs. Carlton brought out an envelope and handed it to Lee. The envelope was addressed to Renee Wilson from Mr. Thomas Marshall, Lee father.

"Hello Ms. Wilson, my name is Mr. Thomas Marshall, Lee's father. I'm writing to let you know that I been taking care of Lee since your mother died. Unfortunaly I too am sick and dying and I'm afraid that once I'm gone, my little girl will be alone. My promise to your mother was that one day, I would reunite her girls again and I would like to fulfill that promise before I die. I'm hoping we could meet and discuss this further."

"Your father located your sister. He wrote many letters to her letting her know about you, how you were doing, everything. Your father kept in touch with Renee concerning you."

Lisa said, *"Wow!"* Lee sat back and took in what she been told. Lisa finally spoke.

"Babe, did you know any of this?"

"No, like I said, my father really never said much about my mom or that I have a sister." Looking over to Mrs. Carlton, *"anything else about my mom?"*

Mrs. Carlton looked serious, *"Did your father tell you why he raised you? Why you weren't with your mom?"*

"That she died," not understanding the question.

"Did he said how?"

"No not really."

Mrs. Carlton took a deep breath and weigh the next statement before she said it. Leaning forward, she put her hand on Lee's lap, finally speaking.

"Dear child, your mom died from breast cancer."

Lee felt like she had been hit in the stomach and it knocked all the wind out of her. *"Why did he feel to keep this from me? Did he feel I couldn't handle it?"* Lee thinks to herself. Lisa grabbed Lee hands and noticed that their sweaty. She rubbed them. Lee looked at Lisa and gave a weak smile.

Taking a deep breath, *"May I ask what my mom name was?"*

Mrs. Carlton smiling, *"Her name was Leigh, Leigh Renee Wilson. Your father named you after her."*

"Wow," Lee trying to get over the shock, *"I never knew he always called me "Lee."*

"Um, let see, yes, you also have an aunt and cousin," flipping through her papers, *"That's all the information I have right now. Would you like to meet them?"* Mrs. Carlton asked.

"Go ahead baby," Lisa coax Lee, *"What's the worse that could happen?"*

"They won't like me." Lee head dropped.

"And if they don't then no big deal. Besides, your sister wants to meet you."

"That she does," Mrs. Carlton add, *"I have her address and phone number."*

Looking at Lisa, *"Will you go with me?"*

Lisa in a reassurance voice, *"Sure, if it's ok with Mrs. Carlton and your sister,"* looking at Mrs. Carlton.

"I don't see why not," she said and handed Lee the paper, *"If you want, I can arrange the visat for you."*

Lee nervously, *"Yeah I would like that."*

"Good." Mrs. Carlton smiled and pat Lee leg.

Mrs. Carlton gathered up her papers and placed them back into the briefcase. Getting up, Mrs. Carlton, with Lee help, put on her coat and headed to the door with Lisa and Lee, turning briefly to face them.

"Don't worry, Renee seems like a nice person. If you have any questions, please call me."

Lee said, *"Ok"* as Lisa said goodbye and watched as Mrs. Carlton headed out to her car and drive off. Going back over to the sofa, Lee and Lisa sat down. Lee looked at the picture Mrs. Carlton gave her and took in everything that happen today. Her mind ran with questions, trying to understand.

"Why didn't he tell me?" Lee asked.

"Maybe he felt you were too young or he didn't want you to worry since he was sick," Lisa said softly, *"But whatever the reason, he felt they were good enough not to said anything."*

Holding the picture in her hands, Lee placed her head in Lisa lap. Lisa stroke her hair. She closed her eyes, the feeling of anxiety faded away.

Chapter Four

It's 5pm when Lee and Lisa sat down to eat. Lisa, who loved to cook, fixed bake chicken with white rice, rolls and a side salad. Halfway through the meal the doorbell rung. Lisa got up to answered it. Coming back into the kitchen with Lisa, it was Kelly and Alexis.

Lee got up and cleared the table after which all four sat down.

"Welcome home dawg," Kelly hugging Lee.
"Good to be home. So how you been?"
"You know me," Kelly started to light up a blunt, *"same old bullshit."*
"Oh no you don't," Lisa looked at her, *"Don't light that shit up in here. You want to smoke that, go home."*
Kelly joking, *"My bad, I forgot you, don't get down like that,"* gave Lisa a smirking look.
Lee quickly changes the subject, *"So Alexis, how have you been?"*
"Ok," she said softly, *"You look good,"* gave Lee a half smile.
"Of course my nigga looked good," Kelly spoke, *"Why wouldn't she? She held herself down in there. She's no punk ass bitch,"* she hit Lee in the arm.

To Lisa and Lee, it was becoming apparent that Kelly had been drinking.

"So how long you on papers?"
"Until I'm twenty-one," Lee trying not to laugh at Kelly who words are slurring, *"I have to go to counseling still and get a job. I can't have any more problems with the law or I go back."*

"Well you know I got your back," Kelly tone started to change, *"Anything you need?"*

Lee amused, *"It's cool, thanks though but me and Lisa got it."*

Kelly fumble for something standing up and almost fell over. *"Yep, she drunk,"* Lee laughed to herself. As Alexis tried to help her, Kelly became agitated and jerked from her falling into the table. Kelly stare at Alexis. Lisa now annoyed, left the kitchen with Lee. Kelly and Alexis still was in there.

Kelly sat back down and went to relight the blunt, Alexis scared, reacts.

"Baby please," she whispered, *"Don't."*
"Don't what?" Kelly snarled.
"Lisa said she didn't want you smoking in here."
"You know what, you're a little bitch, baby don't, baby please. Just shut the fuck up and leave me alone. You always stress someone out."

Alexis sat there and didn't said a word. Lee looked at her and wondered why she put up with Kelly's shit. Alexis wasn't bad looking, dark complexion, mid height, stocky built and wore glasses. She had a beautiful personality, smart but very sensative. Alexis lacked confidents in herself and couldn't see past what she was on the outside not who she was on the inside. Alexis had so much to offer and it was a shame. Lee felt at times felt that Alexis didn't love herself enough. That's why she put up with Kelly shit when most females would have bounced a long time ago. At times though Alexis could and did push Kelly buttons, starting fights for no reason. But abuse was abuse regardless if it was physical, emotional, mental or verbal and if you're not happy why stick around. *Love can't be that blind.*

"Dawg," reached over to Kelly, *"My girl said no."*

"You let her dictate what went on," words slurred, *"Your soft."*

"No, I respect my girl and she said no." Lee said sternly.

At that moment Lisa came back into the kitchen and looked at Kelly in disgust. Kelly being Kelly, started talking shit to Lisa.

"You know what your problem is Lisa," getting up and walking over to her, *"You don't know how to have fun."*

"And what fun is that Kelly? Getting drunk, high or just being an ass."

Kelly took offense to what Lisa said and stopped. Slightly miff, she went back to her seat mumbling *"uppity bitch,"* under her breath. Lisa heard and stepped to her.

"Look, I'm not your girlfriend or one of your hood rats from the street, so in my house you will respect me or you can get the fuck out!"

"Damn girl, can't you take a joke? I was only playing."

"Kelly you have problems you need to solve but like I said, you will respect me. I'm not down for any of your games, now leave my house."

Lee got up and went between Lisa and Kelly. Trying to defuse the satuation, Lee told Lisa to ignore Kelly. Alexis also felt the tension and tried to get Kelly to relax. Kelly felt like she was being "gang" up on.

"Baby please," begging Kelly, *"Let's just go."* Alexis went to help Kelly stand, she grabbed her under her arm. Kelly shoved Alexis hard causing her to fall against the wall and down to the floor.

"Bitch, I said don't touch me!" Kelly screamed.

Lisa shook her head and looked at Lee. *"This is the shit I be talking about,"* she said to Lee. Seeing the satuation about to escalate, Lee went between Kelly and Alexis and got Kelly to calm down.

"Kelly, chill. Your girl hadn't done shit to you."

Kelly looked at Lee half crazy, almost turning on her.

"Lee, she needs to go! Every time she drunk and smoke, she acts an ass," Lisa said pissed.
"Kel," Lee calmly spoke, *"Kel you have to settle down, you're going to hurt someone."*

Lee went over to Alexis and helped her off the floor, *"You alright,"* Lee asked. Alexis you nod yes. Lee noticed she was crying.
"Why you put up with this?" Lisa asked, *"She hits you, cheats on you, disrespects you."*
"Because I love her," walked over to Kelly.
"But you don't deserve this; this is madness to continue to fuck with her."
Looking at Lisa, *"Please don't judge me."* Sighs, *"I'm sorry were not like you and Lee who all lovely and sweet but I <u>do</u> love her and I'm not going to leave just because you or <u>she</u> said so."*
"Alexis, you too smart and beautiful for this, one day, she might just kill you," Lee chimed in.
"Well, that the chance I have to take."

Kelly finally calmed down, looked at Alexis and laughed. To her this was funny. She showed no remorse or apologizes for her actions. Maybe in the morning she would or the next day but for tonight, this was Kelly.

Lee helped Alexis walk Kelly out to her car. Lee put Kelly in the passenger seat while Kelly kept laughing at what happened. Alexis said thank you and sorry and got in and drove home. Lee knew this was not the end of it and by the end of tonight, Kelly won't remember a thing.

Going back into the house, Lee went into the kitchen. Lisa picked up the turned over chair and sat down. Lee pulled up a chair next to her and sat down.

"Lee, Kelly needs help, they both do. Kelly is either going to be jailed, killed or get someone killed. She had major problems."
"I know." Lee sighed, rubbing her face, *"But what can I do?"*

There was no denying that. Everyone knew that when Kelly drunk and smoked, she became a completely different person; like Dr. Jekyll and Mr. Hyde. Lee seen that one night when Kelly got wasted and high and thought this girl from the hood was sleeping with Alexis. Kelly swore up and down Alexis was cheating on her but she wasn't. The girl happened to be a co-worker of Alexis. Kelly didn't want to hear it though and that night when Alexis and the girl were in the apartment together, Kelly came in and started cussing them both out.
"You fat hore! You want to screw around on me!"

Alexis was trying to walk away before things got out of hand. She kept telling Kelly nothing happened and to go on to bed.

"Don't walk away when I'm talking to you!"

21

"Kelly go on. You're drunk, you're making a complete ass out of yourself."

Alexis walked into the kitchen with Kelly right behind her.

"Said you weren't doing anything in here."
"I wasn't," she'd turned to face Kelly.
"Liar."

Next thing anyone knew, Kelly punched Alexis dead in the face. Alexis hit the floor and quickly went into a fetal posation. Kelly was kicking her and hitting her in the back of the head.

"Kel!" Lee shouted.

Lee ran over and grabbed Kelly and slammed her into the wall. By the time it was over, Alexis right side of her face was swollen. Her right eye swollen shut and she had a busted lip and nose. She had bruises on the back of her head, right side and back. The police was called but before they got there, Kelly had already left and Alexis didn't want to file charges against her. Lee and Lisa took Alexis to the hospital where she had a concussion and bruise ribs.

This was the first of many beatings and not to be the last. The last time they got into it, Kelly beat Alexis so bad that Alexis had to be hospitalize for two weeks. When her sisters found out what happen, they went looking for Kelly. They wanted her dead and for one month, Kelly went into hiding until everything blew over.

Alexis had found Kelly cheating on her. Other girls have called the house and even been bold to come by while she was home asking for Kelly. No matter what though, Alexis stayed and when she did go, she always came back. Everybody wonder what kind of hold Kelly had over Alexis. Only Alexis really knew.

"I'll talk to her tomorrow when I go over to her apartment."
"She's not allowed back over here."
"I know, I know. I'll talk to her."
"Please be careful."
"I will."

Turning out the kitchen light, Lee and Lisa headed off to bed after Lee locked the front door. As Lee lied in bed, she had trouble fallen asleep. Her mind was wondering on today events. First day home and all ready excitement. Not so much Kelly and Alexis, that was normal or what some might consider normal. It was her sister and birth mom. For Lee, that was a whole new world. Sometime this week or next week, she would meet the other side of her family. Even saiding that was weird. Would they like her or better yet accept her. Not because she was in juvenile, that didn't bother her. What was keeping Lee up was would they accept her when they found out she was gay.

Lee rolled over and looked as Lisa slept. Pulling close to her, Lee held her tight and tried to fall asleep.

Chapter Five

It was Friday morning and Lee headed over to Kelly's and Alexis apartment. The apartment was only three streets over and Lee decided to walk to clear her mind.

After about twenty minutes, Lee arrived at the complex. The building was a rundown housing unit with four units inside. The bottom two units were empty and mainly got used for storage. The top two house, an elderly black man in one and Kelly and Alexis in the other.

Lee climbed the stairs and enters into a dimly lit hallway. She walked a few feet and knocked on a door. Alexis answered and let her in. As Lee stepped in, she noticed Alexis face was bruised on her right side and her bottom lip was swollen. Lee asked her what happened as she took a seat and Alexis told her they got into it again when they came home last night.

"I'm alright. Kelly just stressed out, you know. No money, no job. You know how it is."
Lee looked at her and shook her head, *"Yeah I do but it doesn't make what she does right. Why do you put up with it anyway?"*
"Lee, you know I don't see myself as pretty or smart. I'll be the first to admit that I got low self-esteem. But I'm not you or Lisa and right now, Kelly is the only girl who will look at me."

Alexis dropped her head. Lee not sure what to said next took her time.

"Just because you're not me or Lisa doesn't mean you're a bad person or ugly," smiled at her. "Y*ou're a very*

beautiful person and have a beautiful personality. You deserve
better than what you're getting."

Alexis looked up at Lee, smiled and said thank you.

"She might be my best friend and all but right is right
and wrong is wrong and Kel is wrong. Lex, I know you love her
but you got to love yourself first. I'll talk to her."
"Thanks Lee, honestly you're the only friend she's got."

A few minutes later, Kelly came in. Her clothes
disheveled, and a wide cut was going across her face; Lee could
tell she had a bad night. Kelly saw Lee, smiled and flopped
down beside her in a beat up old chair.

"So looked who decided to come down and visat," mock
Lee. *"Your wife let you come out and play I see."*

Kelly reeked of alcohol and her eyes are bloodshot red.
She looked like she hadn't been to sleep in the last twenty-four
hours. As she sat, she lit up a joint and smoke.

"So what happen?" Lee nod at Alexis who now took a
seat in the kitchen.
"Oh you know me, when I don't want to be bothered,"
she took a hit and offered Lee a hit who shook her head no.
"So is Lisa still mad at me," Kelly blew smoke into the
air.
"Lisa doesn't want you back at the house after last
night. Kel, you disrespected her not to mention me."
"Well, I didn't lie, she is an uppity bitch. But if that's
how she wants it, cool," she said blowing it off. *"I ain't got to*
be where I'm not wanted."

Lee shook her head. Kelly took another hit then put the
weed out. Getting up, Kelly went into the bathroom. Alexis

came out the kitchen and asked Lee if she wanted something to drink. Lee declined and Alexis went back into the kitchen and started doing the dishes. Lee took a moment and went to look around the apartment.

The apartment was a one bedroom with bath, living room and small kitchen. The living room had one blue beat up chair and black sofa. In the middle of the floor was a black table that sat uneven. The living room floor was cluttered with clothes, shoes, papers and books. Sitting against the south wall was a two tone beige and brown lamp.

The kitchen had a small brown table with yellow and orange chairs. The cabinets were old with the handles falling off and the doors hanging loosely on the hinges. The paint on the walls was chipping and only one light bulb that barely work.

The bedroom sat off the back of the apartment. Like the living room, the bedroom was cluttered with clothes strew all across the floor. Closet door was off the hinges and a big hole in the wall near the door from where Kelly got drunk one night and punched it. A mattress laid in the middle of the floor and a table with an off color lamp sat off in the right corner of the room.

Lee headed back into the living room and looked out the window as her mind wondered. To Lee, Kelly was just *misunderstood*. Same song; she never knew her father and her mom was a drug addict. As a child, she grew up being called "white trash" and "trailer park trash" even though rumor had it that her father was black.

Her childhood was filled with pain and disappointment; molested by her mom boyfriends, her mom constantly abused her either by beating her when she was high or neglecting her so she could go and get high. At times Kelly was left home alone

26

many nights not knowing where her mom was and when she did come home, Kelly was ignored.

One night when she was five, for her birthday, Kelly mom told her she was going to the store to get her a birthday present. It was four days until her mom came home and when she did return she bought her a birthday card that had some else name on it. Not to mention a stale cake. Kelly didn't said anything, just took the "gifts" and went into her room. She couldn't cry though. At an early age, Kelly learned to accept these things her mom did or wouldn't do as a fact of life and bottle her feelings up inside.

At the age of six, she was made ward of the court and sent to live with her grandmother. That didn't work out either. Her grandmother was very religious and nothing Kelly did was ever good enough. Her grandmother was always condemning her for how she dressed or the people she hung out with. Kelly tried though, tried hard but no matter how hard she tried, she couldn't meet her grandmother standard. She couldn't live the life the way her grandmother wanted her to. Kelly ran away at the age of twelve and been running ever since.

Kelly had to grow up fast and take care of herself. Growing up, her mom would said, *"your like your no good father"* or be called "bastard." Her grandmother would said *"you'll end up like your mother, nothing.* Kelly knew in her heart that wasn't true but she couldn't escape that "dark cloud" of what her family said. When she tried to trust people and let her guard down, she got burned bad. Kelly felt like nobody cared about her then screw them.

Kelly found comfort in alcohol and drugs. For a short time, the effects would dull the pain she felt inside. However when the highs were gone, the pain inside was still there only worse.

At fifteen, Kelly dropped out of high school and started hustling to make money. She started out selling weed to friends then moved up to selling heroin, cocaine and crack to the rich kids.

Kelly was at a party with a group of people one night drinking and getting high. At some point (no one ever really been sure about the facts) but later that night, Kelly was slipped a "roffie" and was gang rape. No one was caught. Lee thinks it was after that incident Kelly was pushed over the edge.

When Kelly met Alexis, Lee thought Alexis could help Kelly and be a posative influence in her life. Alexis was the first girl Kelly really loved. Alexis bought to the table, companionship and friendship. She was willing to do anything for Kelly and vice versa. At first Kelly was nice and loving to Alexis but Kelly soon started to change. Kelly past had always been a vocal point in her life; it was always dominated over her.

With the drinking and drugs, Kelly became abusive, first verbally calling Alexis stupid or bitch then physical. She would hit Alexis for no reason. Then Kelly started cheating on Alexis with other girls and staying out all hours of the night. Though no matter how bad Kelly treated Alexis, Alexis stayed.

When it came to Lee though, Kelly treated her with respect. Not many people Kelly let get close to her. Lee was Kelly close and best friend. Kelly looked out for Lee and made sure nobody messed her over. When Lee didn't have money, Kelly would give it to her, even providing her a place to stay when her stepmom put her out.

Kelly would always tell Lee, *"Stay true to you. Don't let what other people said about you change you."* Lee was probably the only one who truly understood Kelly. She felt she owed Kelly for all Kelly done but she also saw what Lisa meant. Taking a deep breath Lee knew she had to talk to Kelly, if not for Kelly then for herself.

Kelly came out the bathroom and sat back down. Alexis entered into the living room and asked if Kelly wanted anything. When Kelly said no, Alexis left out and went into the bedroom, closing the door behind her.

"Kel, you have a good woman in Alexis. Why do you treat her like shit?" Lee asked lighting a cigarette.

Kelly light a cigarette and shook her head.

"Dawg, you got to stop treating her like she doesn't mean nothing to you, I know she does. The other females calling all hours, the cheating, this madness had got to stop. Especially you hitting her for no reason."

Kelly just sat there listening, smoking.

"You know no other females would have put up with you dumb shit this long," laughed. *"They been done left your monkey ass,"* Lee serious now, *"Alexis loves you, I don't know why but she does, try to treat her a little better."*
Blowing smoke into the air, *"Is that what she asked you to talk to me about?"*
"No, not really but you can see it affecting her."
Kelly shrugging, *"She'll be alright."*
"No she's won't. Kel, if you don't change, you're going to lose the best thing you have."
"Ok, ok," puts her cigarette out, *"Anyway what's up with you?"*
Lee finished her cigarette, *"Nothing really, doing this court thing and staying out of trouble."*

"Well anything you need, I got." Kelly stood up and went into the kitchen. Coming back into the living room, she had a Bud Lite in her hand. Sitting back down, she popped the cap off and took a swig before setting the beer down on the table.

"You know, I envy you. After all you went through; you still manage to keep your head up."

"Had to," lights another cigarette, *"Only way to keep from losing my mind. If it wasn't for Lisa though,"* hits the cigarette, *"I don't know what I would have done."*

Took another sip, *"Well, I appreciate you taking that rap for me, you know you're the only friend I got."*

"Like I told you, no problem," gave a reassurance smile.

"But I know it cost you some time. I also know for a minute Lisa blamed me, guess that why she can't stand me now."

Kelly sat there holding her beer, looking into the bottle. Her mood changed. She became somber and humble. As she gently shook the bottle, she saw the beer inside swirl around, just like her life is. Kelly looked up at Lee and smiled then looked back down at the bottle and shook it again.

"You know, no one ever gave a damn about me, they thought I was a waste," Kelly looked at Lee. *"But that never bothered you. That's what made you special, your ability to see past someone faults. Like I always said, never change who you are for anyone."*

"I won't."

"I wish I had what you and Lisa have. You two have something special."

"And so do you and Alexis."

"Na," take another sip, *"Not likes you two. I mean don't get me wrong, I do care about Lex deep down but not like you and Lisa care about each other. I know she'll be there for*

me no matter what but I can't give her what she truly wants;
Trust and unconditional commitment. You got to have those
and me and Lex just don't have that. That's something you and
Lisa have, that's what made it work."

Lee surprised to hear this from Kelly. Lee had never
seen her like this. Kelly had always held in her deepest feelings
for fear of being hurt. This was a first. Kelly was not the hard
person she made out to be but someone who desperately wanted
to open up but was scared to.

"Kelly," Lee reached over to her, *"No matter what,*
you'll always be my nigger."
"Nigga," Kelly laughed. *"For you to be black, you can't*
cuss for shit."
"You got nerve, with your white ass." Lee laughed
back.
"Alright now, I done told you about calling me white,
I'm not white."
"I can't tell."
"Well you know what they said, looked can be
deceiving."
"Whatever."
"Don't get mad cause you cuss like a white girl."

Lee and Kelly continued joking. Finishing her beer,
Kelly got up and took the empty bottle into the kitchen, Lee
followed and stood in the door way. Kelly threw the bottle in
the trash.

"So what's on your agenda today?" Lee asked Kelly.
Turning to Lee, Kelly laughed, *"See that's the shit I'm*
talking about."
"What?" Lee threw her hand into the air.
"Agenda, what the hell?"
"You know what, screw you."

31

"Again, don't get mad at me because you don't have s-o-u-l."

Lee picked up the dish rag and threw it at Kelly who ducked. Kelly begun to mock Lee using hand gestures.

"So what's on you're a-g-e-n-d-a?"

"Nothing really," Lee picked up the dish rag. *"My case worker came out yesterday and told me about my sister wants to meet me."*

Taking a seat, *"So are you going to?"* Kelly asked lighting a cigarette.

"I don't know," Lee said pulling up a chair and sating down. *"Lisa told me I should, so I might. My case worker is going to set up the visat."*

"You should go, what's the worse that could happen?"

Shrugging, *"That's what Lisa asked."*

"So what's the problem?"

"I don't know."

"Question, does she know you're gay?"

"I don't think so."

"And you think," Kelly exhaled smoke, *"She not going to accept you because you're gay?"*

"I guess." Lee looked down at the floor.

"Well if you decide to go, remember..."

"I know, I know," Lee laughed, *"To be myself,"* she nudge Kelly arm.

"See I taught you well," Kelly said getting up. *"And one more thing."*

"What's that?" Lee became suspicious of Kelly.

"Don't embarrass me by trying to cuss."

Lee jabbed Kelly in the arm as Kelly ran out the kitchen with Lee behind her. As Kelly ran into the living room, Lee picked up a small pillow and threw it at her. Kelly picked up the pillow and threw it back at Lee. Lee and Kelly laughed and play fight with each other acting like little kids back in the day. For Kelly, she'd enjoyed herself without the weight of the world on her shoulders; and Lee took advantage of the moment as it took away her worries of meeting her sister.

After a few minutes of having fun, Lee and Kelly sat down and talked some more. Sitting there, Lee realized being around her best friend was what she missed. Seeing Kelly relaxed and having fun, couldn't be described into words. Lee hoped this time never ended and there be more like them with her friend.

It late by the time Lee went to leave. As she headed out the door, Lee turned back to face Kelly who standing there like a little girl desperately searching for approval to know she did good.

"Don't forget, talk to Alexis and what ever is wrong, you two work it out."
"Ok, I hear you. Now go before your wife got mad because I kept you out this late."

Hugging Alexis, Lee headed home. Today was a good day. No problems, no drama, just her and her best friend kicking it like they use to. Lee zips up her jacket and dwells on her talk with Kelly, hoping she and Alexis could patch things up and ponders on her upcoming visat with Renee. Finally arriving home, Lee headed inside feeling good about herself and <u>who</u> she was.

Chapter Six

Lee was at home watching TV. It's Monday afternoon, Lisa was at work and Lee was bored as she flipped through the channels looking for something to watch. The phone rung and on the third ring, Lee answered it.

"Hello...oh hi Mrs. Carlton..."
"Hi Lee...I was calling to follow up with you, see if you had been going to counseling..."
"Yeah, I have a session next Thursday..."
"That's good and how is finding a job going..."
"Still looking...but it's hard though...with my record..."
"Well...I'll see what I can do...you just hang in..."
"Ok."
"Oh...before I forget...I called your sister and she would like to see you this coming Saturday..."
"Ok...what time..."
"Around 1pm...and she knew Lisa will be joining you..."
"Ok...um...do I have to dress for this...?"
(Laughing), *"not if you don't want to...like I told you...Renee is a very nice person...so I'll see you and Lisa around one at Renee home..."*
"Ok...thanks..."

After hanging up, Lee went and sat back down in the chair. That nervous, anxious feeling starts to rise in her stomach. This is it. For the most part, she never really gave it any thought about her mom side of the family. Lee knew only little things about her mom because her father told her a few things. Now at seventeen, she will finally have some sort of closure.

Lisa entered and Lee told her about the phone call and the visat with Renee.

"So are you going?"
"Yeah but I'm nervous."
Smiling, *"it's going to be ok, besides I'll be with you."*

Lee took Lisa into her arms.

"I have told you how much I appreciate you?" Lee
smiled at Lisa.
"All the time," Lisa answered, swaying back in forth in
her arms.
"Have I showed you how much I appreciate you?"
"Not lately."
"Then I think I need to, starting now."
"I agree."

Lee kissed Lisa on the lips. In the background playing
on the radio was *Three Times the Lady* by *Lionel Ritchie*. Lee
and Lisa begin to dance together as the music plays.

"Your once... Twice...
Three times the lady...
And I...love...you...
Yes you're once...Twice...
Three times the lady...
And I...love you...
I ...I ...love...you..."

Lee pulled Lisa closer as they continue to dance. As the
song played, Lee listened to the words, they describing how she
felt for Lisa. How Lisa the only female who captured her heart
and held it. How Lisa been there for her, how Lisa taught her
how to love and what love, true love really was. How there
wasn't anything Lee would not do for her.

"Yes you're once...Twice...

Three times the lady…
I love…you…
I…love…you…"

The week rolled through and Saturday arrived. Lisa was in the bathroom getting dress as Lee stood in the middle of the bedroom floor deciding on what to wear. Lisa stepped out the bathroom. She was wearing demi jeans, a Tommy Hill shirt with blue K-Swiss. Her hair was pulled into a sculptured pony tail. She's wearing a gold necklace with the letter *L* that Lee bought her for Christmas when they first started dating."

Lisa looked at Lee and giggles. Lee was walking around the bedroom looking for something to wear. Lee looked at Lisa and threw her hands in the air in defeat.

"Baby," walked over to Lee, *"it going to be alright."*

Lisa went into the closet and pulled out a pair of black Khakis, a button up orange Polo shirt and a pair of black Tim shoes and hat.

"Here, put these on," she handed the clothes and hat to Lee.
"But babe, I don't know…"
"You'll be fine," cutting Lee off, *"you'll look fine. Now get dress and I will be waiting for you in the living room."*

Lisa head out the room as Lee started to get dress. After she finished dressing, Lee stood at the mirror and looked at herself. She started to second guess the visat. *What if Renee wasn't what Mrs. Carlton said she is?" What if she snuddy?" But most of all, what if Renee doesn't accept her because she gay?"* Lee sat down on the bed, after all these years, this day had arrived. Feelings overcome her: feeling anxious for meeting her sister for the first time; angry cause her father never told her how her mother died, abandon for losing both her mom and father, lost and confuse for not knowing she had a sister and if Renee will like her and curious to see what her sister looked like.

Lee slowly put on her shoes and stood up. After a few minor adjustments, Lee put on her hat and head out the room. Lisa looked at Lee and smiled. Walking over to her she hugged Lee, whispering, *"I'm so proud of you."* Lee gave a sheepish smile back. Lisa and Lee then put on their jackets and head out the door.

Two hours later, Lisa pulled up to a two story brick house in the suburb of town. The house was yellow with a red fence. There was an oak tree in the yard with daisy growing around the tree. Across the yard was a sandbox and a child swing set. A big wheel sat next to the steps, Oakwood furniture sat on the porch.

Lee and Lisa climbed the steps and Lee rang the doorbell. A young lady answered the door and let them in. Inside the house was spacious. The living room had Oxford cream furniture with matching table and lamp set. Along the mantel were pictures, trophies and awards. Below the mantel was a fireplace. A black ceiling fan hangs above the table. The floor had wall to wall beige carpet with different prints. A 25' color TV and stereo sat inside and entertainment shelf with more pictures and nick knacks inside an enclose glass door.

In the living room was the young lady and Mrs. Carlton. Mrs. Carlton was sitting in a recliner chair. The young lady had Lee and Lisa took a seat on the sofa as she sat in a chair across from them.

"Lee, Lisa, this is Renee," Mrs. Carlton introduced.

Renee got up and shook their hands and then sat back down.

Lee took a deep breath before speaking.
"So," hesatant, *"you're my sister?"*
"Yes. It's finally nice to meet you," to Lisa, *"nice to meet you too."*

Lisa nodded and said, *"likewise."*

Renee was 5'5 dark skin complexion with shoulder length hair and brown eyes. Lee noticed a name tattoo on Renee neck and asked her what it said.

"Leigh," Renee smiled, *"that's our mom name."*
"Oh," Lee replied.

Renee noticed that Lee was nervous and asked if she would like something to drink. Lee nodded yes and Renee got up and went into the kitchen. She came back out with two glasses of water and handed them to Lee and Lisa who both said thanks.

"Would you like to see a picture of her?" Renee asked.
"Yes, please."

Renee got up and went over to the entertainment stood and grabbed the photo album and brings it back to Lee. She hands it to her and stood beside her as Lee opens up the album and looked at the pictures. There are pictures of Renee as a little girl on a beach, of her riding a bike and of her in church for Easter in a pink and white dress. There also pictures of different family members. As Lee and Lisa looked through, Renee stood near and explain who the people are.

"This is our auntie and her daughter, and this picture is mom parents but they passed and this is..."

Lee saw a picture of herself as a baby. She was wearing a pink outfit with a matching hat and booties and she slept with her thumb in her mouth. Lisa said *awe* as she looked at the picture with Lee. Lee turned the page and stops; it's a picture of a beautiful young lady, smiling.

"This is our mom," Renee said to Lee.

The lady had beautiful dark skin with long dark, wavy hair. She had a dimple on the left side of her face.

"She is a beautiful woman," Lisa told Lee.
"Yes she is." Lee said softly.
"Would you like to see more pictures of her?"
"Yes," Lee said trying to control her emotions.

Renee flipped through the album and showed more pictures of their mom as a young girl with her parents and sister. There were pictures of her mom as a teenager and young adult. Lee saw pictures of her mom at happier times. Renee showed Lee another picture of their mom holding her. Standing beside the hospital bed was an older, distinguish gentleman.

"That's you," Renee said, *"After you were born."*
"Who is the man next to her?" Lisa asked.
"That's my father." Lee said fighting back tears.

Lee looked at the photo, tears streaming down her face. The photo showed her mom holding a sleeping Lee, happy and lovingly.

"Did she, um," wiping back tears, *"did she know she was sick, I mean, have cancer?"*

"Yes," Renee placed her hand on Lee shoulder.
"It doesn't show."

"Mom was a very strong person. Even though she knew, she didn't let it control her or stop her, life still went on."

"Um, when did she die?"

"A month after your birth," Renee went back to her seat, *"mom called your father and told him about you. At first she was hesatant about calling him because she didn't want to come in between him and his wife but when her cancer got worse, she told him she was dying from it. I guess she wanted him to know about you in case something happen to her. Your father asked mom if he could raise you. To him, he didn't want someone else raising his daughter.*

"How old were you when she died?"

"Fourteen. I went to stay with auntie. She took me in and raised me like I was her own. She helped me deal with losing mom, encouraging me to stay strong. If it wasn't for her, I don't know what would have happen to me. You'll meet her and I hope you like her, she looking forward to meeting you too."

Lee looked at Lisa who mouth "wow." Mrs. Carlton who been quite, spoke.

"Lee is there anything else you like to know," encouraging her to continue on.

"What kind of woman was she?"

"Mom was a beautiful and caring person, who had a lovely personality. She believed life was what you made it, taking the good with the bad. She was honest, if you were right then fine but if you were wrong, then she told you. Mom had respect for those around her and expected the same in return. Mom was tough though, she never made any excuses for herself and never let you do the same. All she asked from anybody was try. She always said, "You never know your true capabilities

until you try." Her faith in God kept her strong; she just never gave up, she was like that way up till she died."

Lee sat there quietly; she doesn't know what to said. She never knew this about her mom. This was a lot to take in.

"I know this is a lot but understand and remember one thing, mom loved you very much. Giving you to your father was the hardest thing she had to do, not because she didn't want to cause she knew your father was a good man and would do right by his child but because she never got to see the lovely person you grew up to be. That was the only regret she had. Right before she died, she told me who your father was and how to find you. Mom made me promise that I keep looking until I was reunite with you, becoming a family again. I'm happy to said that I kept that promise to her."

Lee looked down at the picture of her as a baby in her mom arms. Tears swell back up in her eyes as she begins to understand the sacrifice her mom made, the decision her dad made and the promise her sister kept.

"Anything else," Renee asked.

Lee shook her head no.

"So tell me about you and your friend," smiling at Lisa.
"Well, there not much to said," feeling timid, *"you already know I was raised by my father, his wife put me out when he died. I been in and out of trouble with the law and had a brief stay in juvenile."*
Renee saw her sister becoming uncomfortable, told her it's ok.
"I don't judge people, mom taught me that."
Lee half smiled and continues, *"Um, Lisa here is my girlfriend."*

41

"I know," Renee trying to put Lee at ease, *"Mrs. Carlton already told me. She felt you was apprehensive about meeting me and told me about it, it's ok."*

Turned to Lisa, *"So how long have you and my sister been together?"*

Clearing her throat, *"Three years, I met Lee through a friend of ours."*

"May I ask how old you are?"

Lisa starting to feel nervous herself, *"I'm um, twenty-three."*

"Mrs. Carlton said you been a major influence on Lee. You went to bat to get her sentence reduced and convinced her to get her GED and go to counseling. She also informed me you been with Lee through out it all."

"Yes." Lisa answered.

"Thank you. It's nice to know my little sister had a good friend in you."

"Thank you," Lisa smiled.

A few minutes later, a little boy came through the door. He was dark skin with curly jet black hair. He was carrying a back pack and lunch box and had a huge smile on his face.

"Mommy!"

He run to Renee and gave her a hug. She asked how school was and he answered fine. After he hugged her, he looked around and noticed other people in the room. Looking at Lee and Lisa, he asked her who they are.

"Simon, this is Lee and her friend Lisa," pointing to them, *"remember mommy told you about my sister and finally getting to meet her,"* Simon nodded yes, *"well, Lee is mommy sister, she's your aunt."*

Simon went over to Lee and said hi, shook her hand then Lisa.

"What do I call you," he asked.
"Lee," clears her throat, *"Lee will be fine."*
"Mommy, can I go to my room now?"
"Yes and a little later, I'll fix you a snack and help you with you homework."

Simon said ok and kissed his mom on the cheek and leaves the room.

"He is adorable," Lisa said, *"How old is he?"*
"Seven," Renee answered then turned to Lee, *"how you holding up?"*
"Fine," she replied, *"just taking everything in."*
"Well you have my number and address, your more than welcome to call or come by. I will enjoy that."
"I will enjoy that too."
"We have a lot to get caught up on," Renee said.
"Well ladies," Mrs. Carlton getting up, *if there's nothing else, then this concludes our visat."*

Renee, Lee and Lisa got up and shake each other's hand. Everyone said their goodbyes and Lee and Lisa left. Heading home, Lisa asked Lee how she felt. Lee shrugged and said ok. Today, she met her sister and nephew and seen pictures of her mom and one of her mom and father.

"I wonder if she loved me."

Lisa looked at Lee and grabbed her hand.

"I'm sure she did. Renee seems like she loves you too and happy to finally see you after all these years."
"Yeah," Lee softly

Lee turned and leaned her head back and closed her eyes. Hopefully this would provide some sort of closure for her and a peace of mind.

Chapter Seven

It was Friday night and Club Jazz is hopping. All the locals and people from out of state come to the club for the music and dancers. On any good night the club was packed with patrons, especially on Friday nights to see Lisa, the main attraction. Kelly, who knew the manager from her drug dealings, was there with Lee to see Lisa dance. After a few rounds of Scotch and Cognac both were starting to feel relax.

"Tonight is unusually crowded," Lee shouted over the noise.

"Who cares," finishing off her drink, *"tonight were here to have fun. Bartender, another Cognac,"* Kelly yell, *"and don't be stingy with the liquor."*

The bartender, annoyed, gave Kelly another Cognac and handed Lee a bottle of Michelob Dark. Getting up from the bar, Kelly and Lee go find a table up front and wait for the show to start.

"So I hear you met your sister," Kelly taking a sip, *"how it go?"*

"Ok I guess." Lee replied before taking a drink of her beer.

"So what's she like?"

"Ok," Lee answered.

"Is that all you have to said, "ok," Kelly asked looking at Lee.

"What you want me to said?"

"I don't know," waves her hands in the air, *"is she mean, nice, ugly, what?"*

Laughing, *"Renee ok. We talk, she showed me a picture of my mom,"* took another drink, *"and I met my nephew."*

"And how do you feel after all of this?"

"Ok."

"Damn girl, you need to update your vocabulary."
Kelly said before she finished her drink.

The music started and the DJ announced the start of the
show. The crowd erupted with whistling and clapping as he
spent records. As the music played, dancers came out, one by
one and do their routines.
"Girl you look good...

> *Why don't you back that ass up...?*
> *You a fine mutha fucka...*
> *Why don't you back that ass up...?*
> *Call me big poppa...*
> *When you back that ass up...*
> *Girl who you playing wit...*
> *Back that ass up..."*

"Waitress, another round," Kelly bellowed pointing to
the table.

As the waitress brought over more drinks, the crowd
reacted to the dancers' movement.

"So are you going back over to your sister house?"
Kelly asked between sips.
"I don't know," Lee unsure, *"Lisa thinks I should."*
*"You should. Does your sister know you and Lisa
are..."*
"Yes," Lee took another drink of her beer.
"And," Lisa set the bottle down.
*"She doesn't mind. She appreciates all that Lisa had
done for me."*
"Well Lisa is a good catch."

At that moment, the lights go dim and the overhead
lights begin to circle around the stage. The DJ spoke.

*"Ladies and gentlemen, now for the person you have
been waiting on, who you come out to see, for your
entertainment pleasure, our very own, Ms. Pocoantis."*

The crowd went wild as Lisa came out. Lisa was dress
as and Indian, wearing crouch less pants and a thong. She had a
tomahawk on the side of her pants and was wearing a head
dress with colored feathered.

R Kelly; My Body is Calling for You was playing in the
background as Lisa begins to dance. As the lights shined, Lisa
body glisten as she moves back and forth, her hips swaying like
an exotic snake in a trance. Lisa moved graciously across the
stage, her body limber and flexible. She had a style and class,
different from the others. When she danced, she commanded
respect and got it. She had respect in herself. To her, this was
not about the money; Lisa been dancing since she was a little
girl (her mom had her learn tap, ballet, and jazz), more of doing
what she loved and enjoy. This was what keeps people coming
back to see her. She gave them enough but not too much (like a
stripper). This way she appeased their imagination without
coming off cheap and seeming like a hoe.

"Your girl had a way with the crowd." Kelly said over
the music.
"Yeah," Lee said mesmerize by Lisa.
"Doesn't it bother you?"
*"At first but Lisa told me that's who she is and if I
wanted to be with her…"*
"You had to accept it." Kelly finishes the sentence,
grinning.
"Pretty much," Lee nodded between drunk.

Kelly looked up as Lisa continues doing her routines
and smiled to herself. With every move Lisa made, the crowd
went wild.

"Well, all I can said is Lisa one fine…"
"All right," Lee said looking at Kelly.
"All I'm saiding." Kelly gave her a mischievous look before elbowing Lee arm.

Lisa routine last thirty minutes then breaks. The crowd was on their feet showing their appreciation.

Lee and Kelly head over to the bar to order another drink. As they wait for the bartender, they listen in on a conversation between two men.

"That's one fine bitch." The older man said to his friend.
"Yeah, did you see how she moved," the friend asked, *"made me want to hurt something."*

Lee and Kelly continue to listen, Lee became angry when she realized their talking about Lisa as the two men continue to make derogatory remarks about Lisa. A few minutes later, Lisa went over and orders herself a drink then gave Lee a hug and kiss.

"What's wrong?" Lisa asked sensing something bothering Lee.
"Nothing," Lee mumbled.
What's wrong with Lee," turned to ask Kelly.
"She upset over those two asses." Kelly nodded toward the men.
"Why?" Lisa looked at Lee.
"They were talking shit about you," Kelly answered.
"Oh baby," stroking Lee face, *"that shit doesn't bother me."*
"I know but…"
"And it shouldn't bother you." She'd cut Lee off.

"Told her," Kelly said leaning against the bar drinking.
"I'm a dancer. It doesn't define me as a person though."

"You got to admit though; you have one fine ass body." Kelly smiled at her.

"Shut up!" Lisa said to Kelly who laughing, *"Back to you,"* turned to Lee, *"the only two people that matters to me is my son and you."*

Lisa kissed Lee on the lips as Lee hugged her and kissed her back. Just then the two men at the bar come down and see Lisa and Lee being affected with each other.

"Damn, you're a dyke too," the older man said, *"Still, I can get down,"* stepping to Lisa.

Lee steps off the stool and steps to the guy, fists clinch but Lisa grabbed Lee by the arm and stops her.

Facing the guy, *"First off, your not my type, second, I'm not a dyke, I'm a lesbian and what business is it what I am."*
"Damn girl, my bad."

The older man went to put his hands to Lisa face. Lisa pulled away as Lee steps in front of her. The man friend steps up causing Kelly to step up too as Lisa tried her hardest to get Lee to clam down.

"Chill, I was only having fun, no need to get emotional." The man said to Lee.

Lee jaw became fix and tight. She felt herself stepping out of herself, her heart beating faster and faster, eyes locked into his.

"I was only giving your girl a compliment," he said smiling showing two front teeth missing.

"What ever." Lisa still got hold of Lee arm.

"But," taunting, *"When you want a <u>real</u> man,"* licking his lips, *"call 551..."*

At that moment, Lee snapped. She jerked from Lisa grip and throws a punch straight to his throat. The man stumbled back as Lee followed through with a left fist to his mouth, splitting his lip. Lisa screamed *stop* as Lee continues throwing punched to the man body.

The man friend came around and snuck Lee hitting her in the jaw. Kelly grabbed a beer bottle and hit him across his head, splitting his forehead open. Lee not feeling the affect of the punch staid on her feet and like a dog locked in a dog fight draws blood from his wounds. The man grabbed a bottle and hit Lee across the face. Lee stumbled back and got hit in the stomach. She fell and the man started kicking her in the side. Lisa screamed, then jumps on the man back, digging her thumbs into his eyes, punching him on the back of his head and neck. He threw Lisa aside. Lee getting up, she threw two kidney punches causing him to go down to one knee. Lee, saw Lisa on the ground, became distracted. Going over to her, Lee asked if she alright. Lisa nodded yes and Lee helped her up. As Lee helped her onto a stool, Lisa yelled *"look out!"* Lee turned and felt a pain across her side. She looked down and notice she been stab as blood stain her shirt. In a daze, Lee stepped back then fell to the floor. Kelly who been fighting the friend, saw Lee get stab and go down and came to her aid hitting the man across the back with the bar stool. She took the knife as he tried to flee the club.

Fifteen minutes later, police arrived and begin question the crowd as they disperse. Lisa held Lee and tried to stop the bleeding. Kelly asked if Lee ok, Lisa said she doesn't know.

Lisa looked at Kelly and notice she had a bruise under her eye, a swollen lip and a cut on her cheek. Kelly notice Lisa staring, said she's ok.

Paramedics arrivd and load Lee onto the stretcher for transport to the hospital as Lisa and Kelly follows in Lisa car.

Chapter Eight

In the hospital ER, Lee was being treated for her injuries. Lisa, who had a Band-Aid across her face and Kelly who as an ice pack on her cheek are outside her room talking to the police. Lisa explains how the two men started the confrontation, omitting Lee threw the first punch, and that the older man then stab Lee. After the police got their statement, Kelly headed back into the room while Lisa went and made a phone call. A few minutes later, Lisa came back into the room.

The nurse had finished dressing the knife wound. Lee had stitches going across her forehead and an ice pack to stop the swelling to her jaw.

"Kelly said you went to make a call?" Lee asked Lisa.
"Yeah, I called your sister."
"Why," wincing in pain as Lee sat up.
"Because she's your sister," walked over to the bed, *"and she needed to know."*

Kelly sitting in a chair nodded at the nurse as she walked out the room. Lisa looked at her as Kelly mouth *"what."* Lisa turned back to Lee.

"So how do you feel?" Lisa asked stroking Lee hair.
"Fine, just sore though, how do you feel?"
"I'm fine."
"Dawg," Kelly wheels the chair to the bed, *"you handle your shit tonight, dropping blows, you even shook that punch off from ol dude."*
"I don't recall him ever hitting me."
"Lee, you became a different person tonight," Kelly said getting up from her chair and rolls it over to Lisa who then sat down, *"I never have seen you like that."*

"All I know, he disrespected my girl. I wasn't going to let that shit slide."

"But babe, he could have killed you. It wasn't worth it."

"You're worth it." Lee held Lisa hand.

A few minutes later, Renee and another woman walked in. Looking at Lee, Renee whispered, *"dear God."*

"What happen?" Renee asked looking around the room.

"A fight broke out at my job tonight." Lisa explains to Renee.

Renee walked over to the bed, *"Are you alright?"*

"I'm fine. There no need for everyone to make a fuss like this." Lee said as she readjusts herself in the bed.

"Thanks for calling me." Renee said to Lisa.

"I thought you should know." Lisa responds.

"I'm telling you, my girl ok, she's a trooper." Kelly said, leaning against the sink.

The other woman, who came in with Renee, gave Kelly a funny look.

"And who are you?" The woman asked slightly annoyed.

"I'm Kelly, Lee friend and you?"

Lisa looked at Kelly and said *ignorant* under her breath. Looking at the woman she said sorry and introduces herself.

"My name is Lisa," extends her hand, *"I'm Lee woman."*

"I'm Fannie, Renee aunt," shakes Lisa hand.

Lee sitting up smiled weakly and said hi. Seeing Lee in pain, Lisa readjusts the pillows for her.

Aunt Fannie was about 45, short, heavy set dark skin lady with short gray hair. She is very opinionate and quick to let someone know how she feel and thinks.

"Oh, I'm sorry," Renee turned to Lee, *"I forgot, this is mom older sister, I call her auntie."*
"Nice to meet you, sorry we had to meet like this." Lee gave a weak smile.

Again Renee turned to Lisa and asked what happen.

"A fight broke out tonight between Lee and some guy at my job. Lee was defending me when the guy started disrespecting me.
"What he said?" Aunt Fannie questioned as she looked at Kelly suspiciously.
"He called me a dyke bitch. He was drunk, so I paid him no attention. Lee got upset, they said some words and Lee went off."
"I see," Aunt Fannie said, *"And what did you do while my niece was fighting this man,"* looking at Kelly.
"She fought his friend after he hit me in the jaw." Lee came to Kelly defense.
Renee became more concern, *"Lisa said the man you were fighting, stabbed you?"*
"Yeah, but I'm fine, no big deal."
"No big deal, you could have been killed!" Renee voice raises, *"and what about you staying out of trouble?"*
"The police said because it was self defense, Lee won't get into any trouble."

Renee whispered *"thank God."* Pulling up a chair to sat, Renee asked Lee if there is anything she needs, Lee answer no.

"Dear, what kind of work do you do?" Aunt Fannie asked as she pulled up a chair and sat.

"I'm a dancer." Lisa replied.

"I thought you said the caseworker told you she works at a bank," looked at Renee.

Lisa responded before Renee can, *"I do, during the week. At night on the weekends, I dance."*

"I see," Aunt Fannie looking at her, *"how did you and my niece meet?"*

"Through a friend from work," looking at Lee then back to Aunt Fannie.

"May I inquire how old you are dear?"

Renee looked at her aunt then Lisa and then Lee, a troublesome look crosses her face.

"I'm twenty-three," Lisa showed concern too.

Aunt Fannie direct her attention to Lee.

"And how old are you?"

Sensing she knew where this was heading, Lee took a deep breath before answering.

"I'm seventeen, but I'm legal, why?"

Aunt Fannie getting up walked over to the sink and washes her hands and dries them. Walking back to her seat, she sat down and looked at everyone in the room carefully before speaking.

"The way one lives their life reflects on their situation. If it wasn't for the fact my niece was in a club, a gay club, underage at that, she might not had been hurt."

"What the hell that supposes to mean!" Kelly said reacting to what she heard.

Looked at Kelly, *"I'm saiding, if my niece wasn't gay or if this young lady here,"* points to Lisa, *"wasn't messing with someone half her age, Lee wouldn't be here in the hospital. It's about the company you keep."*

Renee looked at her aunt and said *"auntie"* shaking her head. Kelly who had heard enough jumps up, looked at Aunt Fannie and said, *"bitch please"* and left the room.

Lee looked at Lisa then Renee in disbelieve over what she had just heard too. Sitting fully up in bed, Lee, in pain, swings her feet over the side of the bed and tried to stand.

"Babe, what are you doing?" Lisa reacted as she watched Lee try to stand.

Renee also seeing Lee try to stand up, tried to get her sister to sat back down.

"Sis, please," Renee pleads with her as Lee continues to stand, *"you're going to hurt yourself more."*

"Baby, hand me my shirt shoes." Lee told Lisa.

"Where do you think your going?" Lisa asked.

"Home," Lee adamant.

"You can't, the doctor hadn't release you yet." Renee said trying to hold a shaky Lee.

"I don't care." Lee upset.

As Lisa put on Lee shoes and shirt, and helped her to stand, Lee called for the nurse to come in so she can go home.

Holding on to Lisa, Lee looked at Renee who whispered *I'm sorry* to her.

"Thanks for coming, I appreciate it."

Turning towards her aunt, Lee tried her hardest to maintain her composer.

"As for you, thanks but next time keep your opinions to yourself. You may not like my life style or who I'm with," nodding at Lisa, *"but she's my woman and if you have a problem with that, then that's your hang up, not mines."*

Lee continued to walk toward the door with assistances from Lisa and Renee.

"You know, I was worried about meeting my mom side of the family for this very exact reason," Lee shaking her head, *"but my baby said to go. Lisa been a big part of my life since my father died."*

At that moment, Kelly came back into the room with Lee discharge papers. Seeing Lee up, she went over and grabbed Lee under her arm and helps her. Lee turned to face her aunt.

"Like I said, if you don't like me, fine, I'm cool with that but I'm not going to let you disrespect my girl, I don't give a damn who you think you are!"

Kelly helps Lee walk out the room. Lisa stood in the middle of the floor and looked at Aunt Fannie.

"You know, Lee is really a good person after all she been through. She manages to maintain and keep her head up, even with all the mistook she had made. Lee is strong and

smart with a big heart. You would know that if you talk to her and give her a chance instead of judging her."

Lisa walked out the room leaving Renee and her aunt alone. Renee looked at her aunt and shakes her head.

"Why would you said that?" Renee asked, hurt by what just happen.
"I didn't lie." Aunt Fannie answered defensively.
"Regardless of what Lee is, she is still our family."
"People are going to talk, I'm just stating what there thinking and saying."
"I don't care what other people say. The only thing that concerns me is Lee and how she felt. Look we were giving a second chance with her in this family. If you want a chance with her, you're going to have to accept her for who she is." Renee said agitated.

Taking a deep sigh, Renee went to walk out the room. As she opened the door to exit the room, a sharp pain came across her forehead causing her to stop dead in her tracks.

"Are you ok dear," Aunt Fannie asked seeing Renee in pain.
"Yeah it's nothing, just stress," Renee lying as she continued to walk.

Aunt Fannie knowing she being lied to looked at her and doesn't said anything as she walked out the room behind her.

Chapter Nine

It's been a few days since the incident at the club and Lee was at home relaxing. Sitting outside, the weather was unusually warm this time of season; the temperature is 75 degrees but it felt like 80.

As Lee sat on the front porch, she enjoyed the scenery. Very few people are out except for those who are doing last minute shopping for the upcoming holiday. Some people passing by said hi or wave, while others wished her well.

It's peaceful today with no stress or worries in life. This was what Lee missed being locked up. As she relaxed, her mind wondered. She remembered the sunrises and sunsets, how the stars shine bright on a clear night. She remembered the smell of fresh cut grass or the morning dew, the sounds of birds chirping in the morning, children playing in the afternoon or crickets chirping at night. The sound the wind made and the feeling as it blew or the rain falling as it hits the house. She remembered cookouts and block parties and the laughter of her friends. She remembered most the soft touch of someone you love or who loved you, hearing the sweet soft words of *I love you* being spoken from a person soft lips.

Lee smiled as she reminisced. She knew she was given a second chance, one she will not take for granted again.

Pain in her side brings Lee back to reality. The doctor told her it would be a few weeks for the bruise and soreness to subside. He gave her Tylenol 3 for the pain but afraid she might become hooked, Lee refused to take them.

"There's no sense in you sitting around in pain." Lisa said one day as she watches Lee who was hurting, *"the doctor gave you medicine to take."*

"I'm not taking them." Lee's face grimaces, body hurting from the pain.

"Stubborn. If you're not going to take the pills he gave you then take something."

Lisa went into the bedroom and came back out with two capsules in her hand and hands them to Lee with a cup of water.

"What are these," Lee looked at them funny.
"Ibuprofen."

Lee looked at Lisa who firmly said *take them.* She doesn't move until Lee took the capsules. Seeing Lisa not budging, Lee took them; her face frowns as she swallows them down with water.

"Yuck," she said handing the cup back to Lisa who sat it down.

"Now was that hard?" Lisa laughed, shaking her head.

Lee got up and went into the house and into the bathroom. Inside the medicine cabinet, she pulled out the bottle of Ibuprofen. Taking two capsules, she washed them down with water. Going back into the bedroom, Lee laid down on the bed to rest.

Forty-five minutes later, it's 5pm. After a fitful nap, Lee got up and straightens up the house. Lisa who was getting off work, will be late coming home, she's stopping off at her son father house to pick him up.

After she finished picking up the bedroom and living room, she headed into the kitchen to start dinner. Not one for cooking, Lee fixes hamburgers and French fries. The last time she cooked dinner for Lisa, Lee burnt the food. When Lisa seen it, all she could do was smile at Lee and hugged her.

"At least you tried."

An hour later, Lisa and Quincy walked into the house. Lee headed into the kitchen as Quincy went wash up for dinner. Looking at what Lee fixed, she smiled at her. Once Quincy came in the kitchen, everyone sat down to eat. After grace was said, Lisa fixes everyone plate.

"So how are you," Lee to Quincy, *"long time since I seen you."*
"I'm fine," he replied with food in his mouth.
"Didn't I tell you about talking with food in your mouth?" Lisa asked with a stern look.
"Yes ma'ma," Quincy quietly.
"How was your day?" Lee asked Lisa.
"It was busy, and yours?"
"Ok, I guess."
"Are you home for good?" Quincy took a sip of Kool-Aid.
"I hope so," Lee smiled at him.
"Good, cause I miss having you around," took a bite of his hamburger.

Lee doesn't said anything instead just grins. The rest of dinner was eaten in quite. Twenty minutes later, Lisa got up and puts her plate in the sink to wash.

"After you finish eating, go take your shower and finish your homework before bed."
"Yes ma'ma," he said getting up and putting his plate in the sink.
"Love you mom," hugged Lisa.
"Love you too."
"Love you too Lee," walking over to her to hug.
"Love you champ."

"Goodnight."

Quincy left the kitchen and headed into the room.

Lee washed the dishes as Lisa dried and put them away. Lee took the trash out as Lisa finished cleaning up the kitchen. Afterwards Lisa headed outside where Lee was sitting on the swing.

Lee held Lisa in her arms as they look at the sunset. It was beautiful tonight. The orange and yellowish tip of the sun gracious the skies as it went down over the horizon.

It's quiet. The only sound is a few people talking and crickets chirping. The sky was clear, the moon and stars shining bright. As Lee held Lisa, the swing moves back and forth as the chimes softly chime. Music plays softly in the background;

"Hey baby, let me tell you why...
I can't live my life...without you, all baby...
Every time I see you walking by, I get a chill...You don't notice me but in time you will...I must make you understand...I, I want to be your man; I want to be your man...I, I want to be your man, yes baby I do...I, I want to be your man, want to be you man..."

As the song played, Lee hums the words. She felt relax. Wrapping her arms around Lisa more, she bends her head over and kissed Lisa on the lips.

"I promise not to leave you alone ever again," she whispered into Lisa ear.
"Shouldn't make promises you can't keep." Lisa smiled at her.
"This promise I will try to keep." Lee said.
"I'm going to hold you to that."

"Just don't let go."
"I won't."

As the music continues, Lee softly started to sing the words to the song.

"Words could never explain how I feel; it's so intense, oh, oh, oh, oh...I tried, I tried, I tried to tell you how I feel but I get mixed up (so mix up)...My mind is fine at times I can't see anyone but you...Those other girl don't matter, (no) they can't support my view... I must make you understand...I, I want to be your man, want to be you man...I, I want to be your man, yes I do (baby)...I, I want to be your man, want to be you man...I, I, want to be your man, want to be your man..."

Lisa snuggled up in Lee arms as Lee held her tight.

Chapter Ten

A knock at the door early the next morning got Lee up to answer. It's Renee, Lee lets her in. As Renee took a seat in the chair, Lisa came out the bedroom and said hi. Lisa asked if Renee would like some coffee or orange juice and Renee said orange juice. Lisa went into the kitchen and came out with a glass of juice. As Lisa went to excuse herself to start breakfast, Renee stops her.

"Could you please stay?" Renee asked.

Lisa went and sat next to Lee on the couch. Renee took a sip of juice then clears her throat.

"The reason why I came by was to apologize for what auntie said at the hospital. I wanted you to know it was her opinion, one I don't share."
"You didn't have to do this." Lisa replied.
"No, my aunt action was uncalled for at that moment and unnecessary. I told her that right after you had left the hospital."
"Well thank you, we appreciated that," Lisa said, *"Now if you excuse me, I have to go get breakfast started."*

Lisa got up and went in the kitchen. Renee got up and went over to the mantel and looked at the pictures. Lee watches her sister closely.

"She's a very beautiful person, inside and out," Renee said as she turned to face Lee.
"Thank you," Lee said, *"she had her moments though."*

Renee smiled and took another sip of her orange juice. Going back to her seat, she sat down and places the glass on a cocer.

"Is there something else you want to talk about," Lee sensing something else is on her sister mind.

"Can I ask you a personal question," Renee looked at Lee.

"Yes," Lee looked at her sister curiously.

"Are you happy?"

The question shocks Lee as she tried to figure out the reason for it.

"Yes." Lee answered.

Taking a deep breath, Renee *rewords* her question; *"Are you happy with who you are?"*

Looking at Renee, Lee tried to understand the question. Seeing nothing to explain one way or another, she finally answered.

"I'm happy being who I am and who I'm with," Lee said, *"Being with Lisa is the best thing to happen to me. She put up with more of my bullshit then anyone. She had been with me from the beginning. Lisa believed in me when no on else had, including me. Do we have our moments, yes, all couples do, but we talk. We figure it out together."*

Renee sat and took in what her sister said. She pondered over her next question carefully before asking.

"Are you happy being a lesbian?"

"There it is," she thinks to herself. Renee reading her mind quickly explains the question.

"Please don't get what I said wrong; I don't care about your lifestyle, which is true. I only care about you."

Choosing her words carefully, Lee spoke softly but direct and bluntly.

"When I told my father I was "gay," my father told me how things would change for me. He told me people who were my friends would stop and that society wouldn't accept me for me. He told me that it was dangerous, morally wrong and that it was a sin against God but he also said, "no matter what, you're my daughter and I will always love you." Kelly always told me to be me and not let nobody else dictate who I am, I don't. Kelly had my back, always had. She's my best friend. Now she might be a bit much to handle but she doesn't pull any punches, she keeps it real. If she doesn't like you or the satuation, she'll let you know without a problem. Up until now, Lisa and Kelly been the only family I known, I have. I know people have their opinions about me and what they think I should be. I'm cool with that. What I'm not cool with is someone judging me before they get to know me. I feel that we are all humans and we have a right to live how we want to live and that the only person who can judge us is God."

"I understand." Renee said sounding empathetic.

"So please don't ask me to change who I am, I won't."

"I would never do that," Renee smiling, *"I see Lisa and Kelly means a lot to you.*

"They are."

"Well, I only hope one day you can see me as part of your family too."

"I hope too."

"I know mom would want that."

Lisa stood in the doorway of the kitchen announces breakfast is ready. She asked Renee if she would be joining them. Renee answered no and got up to leave. Putting on her jacket, Renee headed to the door with her sister.

"Are you sure you don't want to stay and eat, my baby can throw down in the kitchen."
"I'm sure but thanks. Thank you for your hospitality."
"Your welcome, please come by any time."
"Thank you."

Renee gave her sister a hug and headed out to her car. Lee stood in the door and waits until she got in and drives off. Closing the door, Lee headed into the kitchen where Lisa and Quincy are already sitting down to eat. Lee sat down as Lisa fixes her plate.

After breakfast, Lisa told Quincy to get dress so she can drop him off at school. Lee clears the table and starts to wash the dishes.

"Thank you." Lisa dried the dishes.
"For what?"
"For what you said to your sister."
"I meant every word."
"I know."

Lisa turned and kissed Lee and then went to get dress. Half and hour later, Lisa came out the room wearing a black skirt with a split in the back, white blouse and black stockings with black heels. Lee is in the living room cleaning up.

"I'll be home early," she said.
"I'll have dinner waiting," Lee joked.

Lisa looked at her and nodded her head laughing. Calling Quincy to come on, Lisa grabbed her briefcase. Quincy came out with his backpack and high fives Lee.

"See ya," he said heading out the house.
"Please try and get some rest."

"I will, I will and you have a nice day at work."
"Thanks, love you."
"Love you too."

Lisa headed out, as Lee stood in the door waving at them. She closed the door and went back to straighten the house and took out the trash. When she was done, Lee took a shower and got dress putting on blue jeans and a maize and blue shirt with blue Nike's.

Heading out the house, Lee went for a walk. With no particular destination, Lee just walked, stopping to window shop, speaking with a few people.

A few miles away, she came to a city park. Taking a seat on one of the park benches, she watched as children play and the elderly feed the ducks and squirrels. Sitting there, she relaxed her mind.

After sitting in the park for two hours, Lee headed home. With the sun going down and the wind starting to pick up, Lee zipped her jacket and stuffed her hands into the pockets. Still feeling sore, Lee took her time walking. Halfway home, she stopped at a store and bought a pack of cigarettes. Lighting up one, she continued on, arriving home a short time later.

Inside, Lee took off her jacket and headed into the bedroom. Seeing Lisa in bed, Lee climbed in bed next to her.

"Where you been?" Lisa inquired.
"I went for a walk then stopped at the park to watch the ducks."
"Aren't you a little young for that," Lisa rubbed Lee's arm, *"are you ok,"* seeing Lee not her usual self.
"Yeah, I'm ok," Lee turned the TV channel, *"why?"*
"It's like you're distant, like something on your mind."

"I'm ok," as she lies back in Lisa arms.

Lisa held Lee as she watched TV. Lisa played in her hair, gently pulling on her braids. Seeing Lee was tense, Lisa massages her temples.

"What you doing home so early?"
"Wasn't busy today, so I decided to work half a day and come home," massaging Lee neck.
"Oh," still flipping through the channels.
"Baby what's wrong?"
"Nothing," Lee sat up in bed.
"We never had any secrets."
"I know." Lee sighs.
"So?" Lisa pushed Lee to talk to her.

Now sitting on the edge of the bed, Lee got up and went look out the window. Staring out, Lee thinking about what her sister said. She tried to find the right words to explain to Lisa what's wrong. *"Why do I feel myself questioning who I am,"* said to herself.

Taking a deep breath, Lee turned to face Lisa as she leaned against the window.

"Baby, what is it?" Lisa saw her facial expression.
"Are you happy with me?" Lee asked.
"Yes," looking confused, *"why?"*
Are you truly happy with me?"
"Yes," Lisa again answered, worried now, *"why?"*
"Something Renee said or better asked."
"What," Lisa moving to the edge of the bed, *"I only heard the end of the conversation."*
"She asked me if I was happy being me."
"I don't get it."
Exhales, *"she asked me, if I was happy being gay."*

"Ok," Lisa said, *"what did you tell her?"*
"I told her I was."
"So what's the problem?"
"I don't know rather I can't explain."

Lee sat back down on the bed next to Lisa.

"Try, what else did she said?"
"Nothing really," plays with her hands, *just if I'm happy with you and other people opinions."*
Reaching out for Lee shoulder, *"Babe, how do you feel about it?"*
"I never really gave it any thought. Yeah, I was nervous about what Renee thought about me being gay but…
"But what?" Lisa questioned.

Looking up to Lisa, Lee pause then continued.

"It does bother me when people said gay or "dyke."
"But why?" Lisa asked again.
"Because," played nervously with her hands.
"Because what?"
"That's not what I am."

Lee hits the bed with her fist.

"Then who are you?"
"I don't know."

Lisa reached out and grabbed Lee's hand and gently squeezed them. Lee looked at her and saw her smiling.

"Baby, only you know who you are and you have to be content with that person. When I came out, I was called every name in the book; lesbian, dyke, gay bitch, whatever. I admit it hurt to think that's what people thought of me but it was their

opinions. I had to learn that. I realize that I was who I am and no one was going to change that, I accept me for me. Now when other people talk, I ignore them, like the man at the club. That was his hang up, not mines. I'm cool with who I am."

Lisa still held Lee's hand gently caressing them.

"Baby, it's not about heterosexual or homosexuality, it's about individuality and what ones feel inside. If two people love each other truly, then who gave a damn what society thinks or said."

Lee didn't say anything. Instead she sat quietly in thought. Getting up, she paced back and forth in the bedroom. Lisa watched patiently. Lisa knew Lee had a lot on her mind. She knew that other people opinions of Lee affected her and Lee held in her feelings instead of expressing how she felt. Lisa got up and walked over to Lee who now standing by the dresser.

"Baby," Lisa reached for Lee's arm, *"I'm with you because I choose to be, I love you."*
"I know," Lee said softly, looking down at the floor.
Lisa Lee's lifted her head up to eye level, *"That's something you never have to question. I hope you honestly feel the same but I can't tell you how you should feel; only you know that."*

Lisa kissed Lee and then hugged her. When she pulled back, Lisa saw Lee crying.

"Oh baby," Lisa said wiping the tears away. *"It's going to be alright."*

Lisa held Lee as she cried. All the pressure that been building up, Lee finally let go.

"I'm always here for you." Lisa whispered in her ear.

Lisa and Lee sat back down on the bed as Lee continued to cry. Lisa held her in her arms and rocked her gently like a baby.

Later that night, Lee eased out of bed and went to sat in the kitchen. With a cup of water in front of her, Lee stared into the cup as she tried to clear her mind.

"God," she whispered, *"I don't know how to feel. I know deep down that I do love Lisa, she's my heart, she's my best friend. But I want my sister to like me and I don't know if she does or just sparing my feelings. I know my dad had his reason as well as my mom."*

Lee sighed as she continues looking into the cup.

"I just want to be me, why is that so hard."

Getting up, Lee poured the water out, turned out the light and went back into the bedroom. Lisa was still sleep. Sitting on the edge of the bed, Lee looked at her and smiled. Easing back in the bed, Lee laid on her back, and looked up at the ceiling with her hands on the chest. Closing her eyes, she tried to get some sleep.

Chapter Eleven

Saturday morning and Lee headed to her sister house. She felt good today; her case worker called yesterday and told her she had a job. Lee will be working in a warehouse loading and unloading electronics. The pay was $9.00/hr. getting paid every two weeks. She would be working from seven to five Monday thru Friday. Mrs. Carlton told her she would help her open a saving account if she wanted.

Lee felt real good about herself. Now she could help around the house now even though Lisa said she didn't mind. Still, Lee wanted to do her part and not have to depend on anyone.

Lee got off the bus. She walked two blocks before coming to Renee's house. Walking up the steps, Lee rung the doorbell. Inside she heard her sister voice said *"coming."* A short time later, Renee unlocked the door and let her in.

Having her sister take a seat, Renee asked if she liked something to drink. Lee said water and Renee went and got it. Coming back, Renee had two glasses of ice water and handed a glass to Lee. Lee said thank you as she took the glass from her sister. Renee took a seat on the couch as Lee sipped her water.

"Nice to see you," Renee said, *"You look a lot better since the last time I saw you."*
"Thanks, I'm still sore though," awkward smile, *"I hope it was ok to come by?"*
"Of course, I was just doing some laundry."
Taking another sip, *"Where is Simon?"* she said looking around.
"He's at his dad's. Every Saturday, his dad come and get him."
"Lisa son, dad does that too."

"How old is her son?" Renee asked as she drunk her water.

"He's six."

"Does he know that you and she are a couple?"

"Yeah, he's ok with it. We don't do anything in front of him. We have that much respect for him."

"That's good." Renee smiled at her sister.

The laundry alarm went off and Renee excused herself and left the room. Lee got up and walked around the living room looking at the different items. Lee ended up at the mantel where she looked at pictures of her mom. Renee with her son and awards and certificates from school. *"She was a beautiful woman,"* Lee thought to herself, *"I wonder if life would have been different if she had lived."*

Renee came back in with the clothes basket and sat down and started folding them. Lee came out of her thoughts when she saw Renee.

Renee saw Lee looking at the pictures of their mom, smiled as if reading her sister's mind.

"Things probably would have been different for the both of us."

"How so?" she asked looking at her sister.

"Well for one, you wouldn't have felt as if you were alone."

Lee gave a sheepish smile and went sat back down. Taking another drink of water, Lee started to feel that nervousness build up. Renee sense it.

"It's weird for me too," Renee said folding shirts, *"But I think we can get through this if we give each other a chance."*

Smiling, Lee nodded in agreement.

"So did you imagine this day would come?" Lee asked.

"Sometimes, other times I really wasn't sure," Renee explained. *"I knew I had a little sister but I didn't know where. The only contact I had about you was from your father. He sent me letters about how you were doing in school and on your birthday. He pretty much kept me informed."*

Renee stopped and took a drink of water; she waited for Lee to take this in.

"But why, he didn't know you?" Lee confused.

"He probably felt he owed mom. In one of his letters, he told me that mom had him promise her he would try to reconnect her girls when she died."

"Ok."

"In his last letter he wrote to me, he informed me that he was sick and was dying."

"My dad was a diabetic; he was in his final stage of kidney failure." Lee said sadly.

"Yes, I know. He was afraid that once he was gone, you have no one. I guess your step mom didn't care for you?"

"She didn't." Lee replied.

"Well, he told me how to get in touch with you when he died. After his death, I called the number he gave me but a woman answered and told me you didn't live there anymore."

"She put me out after my father died," Lee said softly.

"I'm sorry to hear that," Renee showed compassion.

"No big deal, I stayed with Kelly then Lisa."

"Well, I tried to find you without luck. Then a few months ago, your caseworker called me. She told me what happen to you and would I be willing to see you finally."

"I was nervous about meeting you," Lee said, playing with her hands.

"I remember, but I still don't get why."

"I didn't know you and wasn't sure if you like me."

"Because you're a lesbian, right," Renee looked at her sister.

"Well, yeah."

"Like I told you, I don't care about that. I only care about you."

"I know," Lee smiled at Renee.

"And to ease your mind, mom wouldn't care either. As long as you're happy, that's all."

Lee smiled and took another drink of water. Feeling a little more comfortable with her sister made her feel better. She knew that her father kept in contact with her sister and tried to reunite them. This information made her beam inside.

"I hope that helps?" Renee asked.

"It did, thanks," Lee said happily, *"Um, may I ask you a personal question?"*

"Sure," Renee said, finishing the clothes.

"Why didn't you and Simon dad get married?"

"Good question," Renee said shocked, *"Let see, I think I wasn't in love with him, one. I mean I cared about him because he's my son father but my feelings for him didn't go that deep."*

"Did he want to get married?"

"Yes he did."

"Was he upset that you said no?

"No, he was ok with it. I explained to him that I didn't want him to feel obligated because we had a child together. That's how problems arise. I feel, if two people aren't committed from the go, then why fake it. He understood that and because of that we are the best of friends. He doesn't have a problem with doing for his son or providing for him. This way everything works out."

"Do you regret raising your child alone?"

"No, because I know I got support in his father. When it came to Simon, we parent together."

"How does Simon felt about this?"

"Well he's too young to fully understand, and he knew mommy and daddy loves him much."

"Does it hurt that mom not here?" Lee asked.

"It does. Mom missed her first grandchild birth, but auntie was right there so it took away some of the pain from not having mom around."

Lee sat quiet for a minute not knowing what to say. Renee sensing this spoke up.

"It's ok to ask me anything," Renee gave Lee a reassuring look.

"How did you manage with everything that happened?"

"Well," Renee smiled, *"I didn't give up for one. Mom raised me to not dwell on things that had happen or that I could not control. When she was sick, she never let that stop her; she knew that someone was depending on her. I'm the same way. My son depends on me."*

"But aren't you scared you are going to make a mistake?"

"Yes, but that's life. I was taught that it's ok to make mistakes as long as you learn from them."

"Ok."

"Mom taught me that we are all humans but that each one of us had his or her inner strength."

"I wish I had that inner strength right now."

"You do, look how far you have came. Sis, I know that all of this right now is hard to adjust to but you got people who care about you. When things get rough, were there for you."

"Thanks."

Renee leaned in and hugged Lee.

"Now my turn to ask questions," Renee smiled at Lee.

"Ok, what you like to know?"

"Tell me about you, your likes, dislikes, you know."

"I don't know," Lee rubbed her hand across her jeans.

"Well for one, why are you so nervous around me?"

"Well I guess it's because I'm different."

"Clarify," Renee looked at Lee.

"You know, I'm the one who was in juvenile, didn't graduated," Lee looked down at the floor.

"Sis, I keep telling you, I don't judge, we all make mistakes. Look at me, I had a son out of wedlock. We all have to live our own life though."

"I know, but my life been so fucked up after my dad died. When he was alive, we did things together, like go to the park, go to ball games, talk, he made me feel like I was special. When he died, I felt alone."

"Well you have Lisa and Kelly," Renee looked at her.

"I know, but I still miss my dad."

Renee reached out for Lee hand, "I know how you feel."

"Does the pain go away?"

"In time, but never let go of the good times with him, they keep you through the bad times."

"Yeah," Lee suddenly remembered, "Oh I almost forgot the reason I came over here."

"Oh, what's that?"

"I got a job."

"That's good, what will you be doing?"

"Working in a warehouse, um, Franks Electronics. I'll be loading and unloading electronics."

"When do you start?"

"Monday morning."

"Well, I'm proud of you. See everything is turning out ok."

"Yep," Lee beams with pride.

"Does Lisa know?"

"Not yet, I wanted to tell you first."

"I feel privilege," Renee said, happy for her sister.

"Well, I wanted my big sister to know."

"Thank you. I really hope everything works out for you."

Lee got up and put on her jacket.

"I don't want to over stay my welcome."
"You're not," Renee gently hit Lee's arm, *"But thanks for coming by. Come by whenever you want, were family."*
"I will thanks."

Renee hugged her sister goodbye and walked her to the door.

"If you need me for anything, don't hesitate to call."
"I won't."

Lee left and headed home. Her mind still spinning from her talk with Renee. Lee started to feel like she finally belonged somewhere.

At home, Lee fixed herself a sandwich while waiting for Lisa to come home. Sitting at the table, Lee ate in quite.

Twenty minutes later, Lisa came in. She didn't have to be at work until 10 tonight, giving her time to relax. The phone rung and Lisa answered it.

"Hell...oh hi Renee...I just walked in...ok...I'll ask her...I'm sure she wouldn't mind...ok...yes...I'll have her call you...thanks...ok...bye..."

Lisa went into the bedroom where Lee was sitting up in bed watching TV.

"Your sister called," she said undressing, *"She invited us over for Thanksgiving dinner. I told her we would come if that's ok with you?"*

Lee nodded yes as Lisa headed into the bathroom to take a shower.

"*So how was your day?*" Lisa yell over the water.
"*It went well,*" Lee stood in the doorway.
"*Renee said you visited her today?*"
"*Yes.*"
"*So how did it go?*"
"*Fine, I learned a lot from her not only about my mom but my father too.*"
"*Like,*" Lisa said stepping out the shower drying off.
"*That my dad wrote to Renee daily and about the promise he made to my mom.*"

Lee went back into the room, with Lisa following, towel covering her up. Lisa went over to the bed and sat, putting lotion on her body.

"*He kept in touch like that.*" Lisa surprised.
"*Yes. Apparently he didn't want me alone after he died.*"
"*Wow!* Lisa exclaimed.
"*My exact words,*" Lee lotion Lisa back, "*Guess what babe?*"
"*What?*"
"*I got a job.*"
Turning to face Lee, "*I'm happy for you,*" hugging her, "*When do you start?*"
"*Monday morning.*"
"*So are you happy?*"
"*Yep, now I can help you out.*"
"*Baby I don't mind.*"
"*I do though. I want to help you as much as you helped me.*"
"*Awe baby, that's sweet.*"

Lisa leaned in and kissed Lee.

"We have some time before you go to work," Lee was looking mischievous.
"What you have in mind," Lisa kissed Lee.
"Let me show you."

Lee pulled Lisa down on top of her. She kissed Lisa softly, stroking her back. Caressing her breast, Lee slowly kissed her chest moving down to Lisa belly button. Lisa body reacts to every touch she felt. Lee rolled over on top and looked deep into her eyes. She kissed Lisa passionately on her lips causing Lisa to moan with pleasure while stroking her side. As Lee worked her way down, Lisa took her hands and rubbed Lee's back. Lee was gentle with every touch; she took her time wanting this moment to last. She wanted Lisa to enjoy what she had to offer. Lisa took her nails and dug them deeper into Lee's back, her body yearning for more till she reached that climax.

Chapter Twelve

Lee's first day at work was hard. Clocking in at 6:55, Lee's been going nonstop, taking two fifteen minute breaks and an hour lunch.

Lunch was slice turkey breast sandwich on wheat bread, fruit cup, broccoli spears and juice. Lisa fixed her lunch the night before with a small sticky note reading; *have a good day, love* with a smiley face.

Lee boss was an older white man with slightly grey hair. He was pretty lean back. He allowed his workers to have fun as long as they worked. He believed in an honest day work.

Lee wasn't the only female employee that's worked there. There were three others; one black, two whites and a Hispanic woman. They work together but at breaks and lunch, Lee kept to herself.

No one knew that Lee spent time in juvenile or that she's a lesbian. She kept her business to herself. All she did work and that's all they have to know. She was a hard worker.

Quitting time finally came and Lee can't wait to go home. Lee caught the bus home. On the bus ride home, Lee felt good about herself. She finally had a job, her own money. She won't feel like a bothered or strain on Lisa. She can finally take care of business.

Lee got off the bus one block from the house. Walking, she stopped off at the store for cigarettes and a bottle of water.

The weather was becoming cooler, the wind was picking up. Its one week before Thanksgiving. Lee pulled her jacket up around her ears to keep warm and headed home. She lit up a cigarette and smoke it along the way. In fifteen minutes she was home.

Lee took a shower and relaxed until Lisa came home. Twenty-five minutes later, Lisa arrived and headed into the bedroom.

"How was your first day at work?" Lisa asked taking her shoes and skirt off.
"It was hard."
"Did your side give you any problem?" Lisa asked.

Lisa took off her blouse and put on a pair of black shorts and a white tee. She sat back down on the bed.

"A little but I took some Ibuprofen."
"Do you like the job?"
"It's hard but the time went quick."
"Well I see a difference in you," Lisa said getting up, *"I'm happy for you."*
"Thanks."

Lisa and Lee headed into the kitchen to start dinner. Lisa was fixing chicken Alfaro with a Caesar salad. They sat down for dinner having a quiet evening together.

Two weeks had pass for Lee at work. Her boss was proud of her for the hard work she had done. It's Friday, payday. She made in two weeks $568.80 after taxes. Lee headed to the bank to cash her check. She opened a saving account and deposit $270.00. The rest she kept.

Heading home, Lee stopped off at a store to buy one red and one white rose.

Lisa was there when Lee walked in. Walking over to her, Lee gave her a hug and handed her the roses. A huge smile came across Lisa face. She hugged Lee who was standing there beaming.

"Awe baby," Lisa said blushing, *"There are beautiful, thank you."*

"You deserved them for all you done for me." Lee said.

"Baby," Lisa hugged Lee.

"One more thing," going into her pockets, *"This is for you."*

Lee pulled out the money and handed it to Lisa.

"What's this for?" Lisa asked.

"For you, do as you want. I want to start contributing to the household."

"Baby, I told you, I don't mind. I do it for us, I'm your woman."

"I know but I mind. I don't want my woman..."

"Your pride," Lisa cut Lee off, *"I'll take the money and use it for the household. We can contribute together, ok?"*

"Ok, I will put the rest in a saving account today."

"That's good. I'm so proud of you, you have come a long way."

"Thanks, I actually feel like I'm doing something meaningful."

"You are and don't let no one tell you different."

Lee and Lisa sat down in the living room and talked about ways to use the money. Lee suggested a pool table, Lisa said no laughing. They stayed up the whole night talking and laughing for the first time in a long while.

Chapter Thirteen

Thanksgiving Day, Lee and Lisa were getting dressed to go over to Renee's house for dinner. Again Lee was having trouble getting dress. Lisa looked at her and laughed.

Lisa was wearing a long, black skirt with a beige long sleeves blouse, with a v-neck green sweater and black heels. She also was wearing the necklace Lee bought her.

Lee finally picked out something to wear; black Dickies, blue collar shirt with a black jacket and a pair of Nike's.

The drive didn't take long arriving at Renee's home in twenty minutes. Going up to the house, Lee carried a tray of bake macaroni and cheese and a tray of rolls on top as Lisa brought in a dish of green beans casserole. A knock at the door brought Renee who was wearing a blue skirt and a sky blue short sleeve blouse with matching gold necklace and ear rings. Wearing slippers, Renee showed them in.

The living room was set up with Thanksgiving decorations; cut our turkeys on the windows and little Indians and pilgrims figurines on the mantel. In the dining room was a long black hand carve oak wood table with six matching chairs. The table was set with decorative china plates and sterling silverwares on folded napkins, with glasses above the plates.

"You can have a seat," Renee motioned to the chairs.
"Do you need any help?" Lisa asked sitting her dish on the table.
"No, I think I'm alright," Renee said taking the other dishes from Lee.

Lee and Lisa took a seat, as Renee started bringing out the food from the kitchen; turkey, ham, cornbread stuffing, mash potatoes, collards greens, yam, cabbage and for dessert, pound cake and JELLO.

"Will others be joining us?" Lee asked.
"Yes, Simon, auntie and her daughter Keshia," Renee said, *"Her daughter is fifteen."*
"Oh." Lee said nervously.
"It's ok," Renee said seeing her sister reaction, *"Auntie knew you were coming with Lisa and she promised not to say anything about your lifestyle."*

Lee gave a weak smile. She got herself some punch and drunk it down fast. Feeling "hot," Lee excused herself and went outside. Renee looked at Lisa concerned.

"She just worried that's all," Lisa replied, *"I'll go check on her."*

Lisa got up and went outside to where Lee was sitting on the steps smoking. Walking up to her, Lisa gently touched her shoulders. Lee turned around and a smiled as Lisa sat down next to her.

"I wish Kelly was here," Lee said between smokes.
"But she's not, we agreed. Besides you'll do fine, just be yourself."
"What if..."
"You'll be fine," Lisa cut Lee off.
"Is everything ok?" Renee asked coming to the door.
"Yes I'm ok," Lee put her cigarette out.
"Are you sure?" Renee not truly convinced.
"I'm sure."

Lee headed back inside with Lisa and her sister. Going back to the dining room, Lee and Lisa sat down. A few minutes later, the doorbell rung and Renee went to answer it. Coming back into the room with Renee was Simon, Aunt Fannie and Keshia.

"Lee and Lisa, this is Keshia, auntie daughter," Renee introduced, *"And Keshia, this is Lee my little sister."*

Aunt Fannie was in a black slack outfit with matching jacket and low cut heels as Keisha was wearing a cream color dress with matching shoes and small ear rings. Simon was wearing dark color jeans and a grey short sleeve shirt and black shoes.

Everyone said hi and took a seat at the table. Renee was sitting at the head of the table. Next to her was Lee then Lisa and across from them were Keshia and Simon. At the end was Aunt Fannie. Renee bowed her head and said grace.

"Dear Father,
Thank you for allowing us to come together and see another day. Thank you for keeping us safe. We thank you for this food that we are about to partake of. Bless those without. Bless everyone gathered around the table. And Father, thank you for bringing me and my sister together.
In Jesus name, A-Men"
"A-Men!"

Everyone started to dig in. The dining room was filled with laughter and life. Everyone went for seconds and more. Talking and laughing, everyone was enjoying their self.

"Lisa, I was hoping you would have brought you son," Renee said.
"He's with his dad. We switch every other holiday," Lisa said drinking her juice.

"That's good," Aunt Fannie nodded her head in approval, *and "It's nice to see both parents involved in their children lives."*

Lisa nodded and took another bite of her food.

"So sis," Renee spoke, *"How is your friend doing?"*
"She's ok, she spending thanksgiving with her friend."
"Oh, well she was more than welcome to come."
"Naw, she said she wouldn't have felt right."
"Why dear?" Aunt Fannie curious.
"She felt I should be with my family," Lee lied.
"Well tell her I said hi and maybe next time," Renee said between bites.
"I will."
"So Keshia, what grade are you in?" Lisa asked.
"I'm in the ninth grade," Keshia replied softly.
"Ok. What school do you go to?"
"Saint Mark's Private School."
"That's a good school." Lisa remarked.
"Yes, one of the best," Renee said proudly, *"I graduated from there."*
"Oh," Lee sounded surprised.
"What school did you go to?" Keshia asked Lee.
"I went to Clarks High School," Lee answered nervously, *"But I didn't finish, I dropped out."*

Lee looked down at her plate feeling ashamed.

"So you didn't graduate?" Aunt Fannie inquired more.
"No, instead, I got my GED."
"Oh."
"May I ask why you quit school?" Aunt Fannie looked at her.
"I guess I felt I wasn't smart enough."

"But that doesn't mean she's dumb," Renee was coming to her sister defense, *"Lee still smart and talented."*

Renee smiled at Lee causing her to blush.

"From what I understand, she likes to write and even dapples in music." Renee said proudly.

"How do you know that? About the music?" Lee looked at Lisa who shook her head.

"Your father told me," Renee was still beaming with pride.

"He told you that?" Lee was shocked.

"Yes, he sent me pictures of you in the church choir and musical concerts at school, said your favorite instrument was the violin."

"I never knew."

"Your father was proud of you, and he wasn't ashamed of letting people know. He knew you had potential even if you didn't. Lisa and I are proud of you and if mom was here, she'd be proud too."

Lee didn't say anything. Trying to fight back tears. He never shared any of this with her as she wondered why. Wiping back tears, Lee looked at Lisa and smiled. Lisa squeezed her hand and smiled back. Lee looked at Renee who nodded with approval. Lee felt she was going to make it after all.

Dinner was done and everyone helped Renee clear the table. Aunt Fannie and Renee were in the kitchen washing and drying the dishes as Keshia and Lisa finished cleaning up the dining room. Lee and Simon took out the trash.

"I still think it's wrong," Aunt Fannie whispered to Renee, *"That Lee and Lisa are, you know..."*

"Lesbians," Renee responded, *"Auntie, that's their life and if their happy..."*

"It's still wrong," she state adamantly.

"Why because you said so?" Renee stopped and looked at her aunt.

"No, the BIBLE said so." Aunt Fannie being direct.

"Doesn't the BIBLE also say something about judging people?"

Renee smiled as she continued to dry the dishes. Caught off guard, Aunt Fannie turned beet red and didn't say a word. She continued washing dishes.

"Auntie, she's my mom daughter, my sister and your niece. Why is it so hard to accept her as she is?"

Aunt Fannie still upset didn't say anything.

"Did you love mom?" Renee looked at her and asked.

"Of course I loved my sister."

"No, I mean truly love mom, in spite of the mistake she made?"

Aunt Fannie was shocked at the question she was being asked.

"You know I loved you mom."

"Do you love me, in spite of my flaws?"

"You know I love you, why you asking these questions?" Renee took a deep breath, *"Do you love Lee?"*

Putting the dish towel down on the counter, Aunt Fannie looked at Renee. She didn't say anything, just stared at her trying to understand the reasoning behind the questions. A few minutes pass by before she finally spoke.

"You and Lee are my blood, yes. Your mom was my little sister, my best friend who I miss daily. I loved my sister with all my heart. So yes I do love Lee the same as you. However, I do not have to accept something I don't believe in or know is wrong and homosexuality is wrong according to GOD Word."

"But auntie, if God can accept her, I don't get why can't you."

"Baby I'm sorry, I do accept her as my niece but I can't accept what she does."

Aunt Fannie went back to washing dishes. She started humming to herself, "I Don't Feel No Way Tired."

"Your mom sure loved this song," Aunt Fannie said, *"She sang this song over and over the day she found out she had breast cancer. She said even in sickness, God still had a plan for me. She refused to let her cancer beat her."*

Aunt Fannie continued humming, and then softly sung the words:

> *"I don't feel no way tired*
> *I come too far from where I started from*
> *Nobody told me, the road would be easy*
> *I don't believe he brought me this far to leave me."*

Aunt Fannie started feeling a joy overcome her. A joy of comfort and hope. As tears streamed down her face, she continued singing the chorus:

> *"I don't feel no way tired, Lord*
> *I come too far from where I started from*
> *Nobody told me, the road would be easy*
> *I don't believe, he brought me this far, to leave me."*

As she kept singing, Renee smiled as she listened to her aunt sing. Renee loved it when her aunt sung; it reminds her of her mother, and how her mom would sing to her when she was a child.

Renee continued to listen when suddenly; she made a chilling scream and dropped a glass into the sink shattering it. Grabbing her head, Renee doubled over in pain.

"Child, what's wrong?" Aunt Fannie scared.

The rest of the house came hurrying into the kitchen as Aunt Fannie helped Renee over to a chair. Lisa wet a towel and handed it to Aunt Fannie who placed it over Renee's forehead. Lee poured her sister a glass of water and handed it to her.

"What's wrong mommy?" Simon asked seeing his mom in pain.
"I'm fine," Renee said, *"Just a little headache."*

Not convinced, Aunt Fannie stood and looked at her funny.

"Auntie, I'm ok," I'll take a sip of water, *"It was just a migraine, seem like I have been having them lately."*
"Um hum," Aunt Fannie still not believing her, *"That was no migraine noise you made."*
"And you know that how?"
"Auntie knew these things."

Aunt Fannie stood there looking at Renee with her hands on her hips.

"Well, I'm fine, see," Renee said getting up, *"No need to fuss over nothing."*

"I'll be the judge of that," Aunt Fannie said patting her feet, still thinking she was being lied to.

Lisa looked at Lee who was looking at Renee scared. She knew it was more than her sister was letting on.

As night came to an end, Lee and Lisa said their goodbyes and headed home. On the ride home, Lisa commented on what happen with Renee.

"She looked real bad."
Lisa looked over at Lee and saw she wasn't listening.

"Babe, did you hear anything I said?" Lisa touched Lee's arm.
"Oh," Lee replied coming out of her thoughts, *"Sorry, what did you say?"*
"I was talking about Renee and what happen tonight," Lisa looked at Lee, *"Are you ok?"*

Lee looked at Lisa; her expression caused Lisa to be concern.

"Baby, what is it?" Lisa sounded worried.
"Tonight was not the first time that had happen to Renee," Lee said softly.
"What do you mean?" Lisa asked now worried.
"The day I visited Renee, we were sitting around talking…"

Lee had a flashback to that day and told Lisa.

"Well, I'm so proud of you. See everything is turning out ok."
"Yep."
"Does Lisa know?"

"Not yet. I wanted you tell you first."
"I feel privileged."
"Well, I wanted my sister to know."
"Thank you."

Talking to Lisa, *"I remember getting up to leave, then..."*

"Are you ok," Lee asked Renee who doubles over in pain, grabbing her head, *"Sis!"*

Lee rushed over to Renee and leaned down beside her. Renee rubbed her head and Lee helped her up and back into the chair. Going into the kitchen, she came back out with a glass of water and handed it to her.

"Thank you," Renee said taking the water and drinking it, *"I'm ok now."*

Looking at her scared, Lee didn't believe her.

"What happen?"

Lee was still scared and did not know what to do.

"I'm ok," Renee said finishing her water, *"Migraines, they come and go."*
"Are you sure?" Lee said not sounding convinced.
"Sis, I'm ok," Renee answered patting Lee's arm, *"I have medicine I take."*

Not buying it, Lee insisted on calling someone.

"There is no need. Look, if it happens again, I'll call 911."

"I can stay if you want, at least until Simon came home, or I can call auntie."

"There is no need," Renee said trying to sound persuasive, *"I promise you, I'm ok."*

"So you left?" Lisa asked pulling up to the house and park.

"She said she was ok, what was I suppose to do?"

Lee and Lisa got out the car and climb the steps to the front porch.

"I guess nothing," Lisa unlocked the door.

Lee and Lisa went inside the house. Lee closed the door behind her.

"Did you tell anyone?"
"No just you."

Lee sat down on the couch as Lisa took the food into the kitchen. She came back out and sat down next to Lee.

"After tonight, you should tell your aunt this happen before."

Sighing, *"Renee doesn't want me to."*

"But Lee, this is serious, Renee could really have something wrong with her."

"I know," Lee rubbed her face.

"So what are you going to do?"

Lee got up and went into the kitchen and poured a glass of juice to drink. Standing over the sink, Lee drunk the juice and then put the glass into the sink. Lisa followed and hugged her from behind. Lee was afraid; she didn't know what to do.

She hated seeing her sister in pain and not being able to do anything. She told Renee she wouldn't say anything though.

"A person word is all they have. Without it, they have nothing."

Lee's father told her this when she was young.

Turning to kiss Lisa, she said goodnight and headed into the bedroom to lie down.

"Lord, please watch over my sister," Lee whispered before turning over to sleep.

Chapter Fourteen

Sunday afternoon and Lee and Kelly are hanging out at an abdomen elementary school.

This was where they would come to as teenagers to get away from the stress of home life and just sat and drink all day.

Sitting on the monkey bars, they felt the wind as it blew. Lee pulled her jacket in close around her neck, Kelly only wearing jeans, a Michigan sweater and blue skull cap.

Kelly lit up a cigarette and took a puff. Sitting on the ground below was a bottle of Jack Daniel's wine. Jumping down, Kelly retrieved the bottle and took a drink. Climbing back up to where Lee was sitting, she offered Lee a drink. Lee shook her head no.

It's early December and the days were shorter. There wasn't any one out. In the distant, a train whistled.

"So how was your thanksgiving?" Lee asked.

"So, so," taking a puff, *"Alexis fixed dinner, nothing fancy. How was your dinner at your sister?"*

"It went well, my aunt came over with her daughter and my nephew was there."

"A family affair," Kelly snickered sarcastically.

Looking at Kelly, Lee shook her head. Lee lit up a cigarette and smoked as Kelly took another drink of wine.

"Did your aunt start up with you about your life style," Kelly said using her fingers in quotation?

"No, Renee said she talked to auntie about it and auntie promised not to say anything about it."

"Um- hum."

"Really, she was on her best behavior," Lee said using her fingers in quotation.

"I hear ya. I'll believe that when I see it."

"Well, Renee asked about you," Lee said in between puffs, *"Said next time she hopes to see you."*

"Um-hum," Kelly looking at Lee cross eyed.

Kelly finished off her bottle of Jack Daniels and jumped down the bars, sitting on the bottom bar. Lee followed and sat next to her.

Kelly opened up her bag and pulled out another bottle of wine, opened it and started downing it. Lee looked on and calls her "alchie" and laughed at her. Putting the cap back on, Kelly put the bottle back in her bag.

"So what else happen," Kelly said wiping her mouth across her sleeve.

Lee proceeded to tell Kelly about the evening. Meeting her cousin, more about her mom and how her dad kept in touch with her sister and same interest her mom had, she had. Lee also told Kelly about what happened to Renee later on that night and what Lisa said concerning it.

"Lisa right?" Kelly said taking puffs on her cigarette, *"You should tell your aunt."*

Lee, shocked that Kelly would agree with something Lisa said looked at her in disbelieve.

"I know but I promised Renee I wouldn't tell her."

"How would you feel if Lisa or me kept something from you like that," Kelly said becoming serious.

"You know I go the fuck off."

"Then imagine how your aunt would feel when she finds out that this wasn't the first time this happen to your sister and you knew," Kelly said pointing to Lee.

Lee sat quietly. She had thought about it. She knew if her aunt found out, this would add to the already strain in their relationship. Plus Lee would never forgive herself if something bad happened to her sister and didn't said anything. Kelly was reading her mind.

"It's ok to keep promises that you can keep, people will trust you. But those you know you shouldn't keep, don't. Lee, you have a second chance at life. Your sister really cares about you and loves you that was evident at the hospital. She's family now. Do whatever it takes to keep it that way."

"When did this life change come about," Lee said shocked and amazed.

"Who knew? All I know, people like us don't get many chances in life to start over or do something different or better. You're one of the few. Lee, take advantage of it," Kelly pointed toward the sky, *"Somebody up there must really love you to give you another shot."*

"Somebody loves you too," Lee slightly hit Kelly back.

"Please. I raised so much hell, I don't think he cares. I was born alone, I'll die alone," Kelly said in between swings.

Kelly took another puff of her cigarette and drunk some wine.

"But best believe, when I do die, I'll go out being me."

"And ass," Lee laughed.

"Whatever."

Kelly finished off the bottle and got up and threw it across the field. Sitting back down, she finishes her cigarette.

"You're lucky, Lee. Your father loved you enough, that when your mom called, he came and raised you when she died. He even stayed in touch with your sister and told her how to contact you when he died. Not many men I know would have done that. Hell, I don't even know who my father is or where he is or if he gave a fuck. It's cool though, I manage this far without him, and I'll keep managing."

Lee sat quietly and looked at Kelly, she was speechless. Kelly had always had an opinion on life but never been the one on sentiments.

"Kels," Lee said eyeing her suspiciously, *"Are you ok?"*

"I'm ok," she nodded her head.

"I never have seen you like this."

"Like what?"

"This deep, how does Alexis feel about the new Kelly?"

"I don't know we got into a fight and she left," Kelly said sounding somber.

"I'm sorry to hear that."

"Don't be, I'm not."

"Can you blame her though; I mean she put up with a lot of your shit."

"I don't know. Maybe her and I had reached the end of our relationship. Don't get me wrong, I do care about her. It's just Alexis had expectation of what she thought I should be. I couldn't be that, I'm me and I wasn't going to change that for anyone."

"Are you going to be alright," Lee looked at her.

"You know me, I'll manage."

Kelly got up and grabbed her backpack. Hitting Lee's arm, she walked off. Lee looked at her concerned. She never seen Kelly like this but she knew Kelly will be alright, she knew Kelly was a fighter. Lee just wished her best friend would find that inner peace and happiness before it was too late. Grabbing her things, Lee headed home.

Chapter Fifteen

It's been two weeks since Lee talked to Kelly. Word on the street is Alexis finally left Kelly for good. Alexis got tired of the abuse and cheating and moved out and moved in with her sister.

Lee hadn't been spending much time with Kelly either, working overtime for Christmas. This year, Lee wanted it to be special. Now that she's working, she could get Lisa something nice along with her sister and nephew.

Lee managed to save up to $3,000 putting aside half her paycheck. Lisa told Lee about a coat she seen at Macy she wanted. The coat was red, full length wool with cashmere lining in mink. The coat cost $2,000.

"You what," Kelly reacted to Lee decision to buy it.
"I thought you would like it."

Lisa fixes Lee a sandwich and sat the plate down in front of her along with a glass of ice tea. Lisa then sat down next to her.

"You said you been looking at it," took a bite of her sandwich.
"Yeah looking, that coat cost way too much. That money can be spent on something useful but a coat."
"I want to get you something nice."
"I appreciate that but babe, that's too much."
"You deserve it."
"Not a $2,000 coat. I know you want to do something nice for me this Christmas but please don't spend that much money on me, I'm not worth it."

Lisa got up and kissed Lee and headed out the kitchen. Lee sat and finishes eating her sandwich.

Weeks pass as Lee continues to work. Her boss, who compliments her as a good worker, gave her a raise. She now made $10.00/hr. Lee haves confidants about herself, she felt she can do anything she puts her mind to.

Lee told Lisa of her idea of going back to school to study journalism and creative writing. Lisa told her it's wonderful and encourages her to go register for the up coming quarter. Lee calls Mrs. Carlton who told her she'll help her with the paperwork and help her get finical aid. Lee meets with an advisor who informs her when classes start and how much the tuition is.

"The tuition is $647.00 not counting books," Lee explains to Lisa as they do Christmas shopping, *"She also said that if I get the paper work in, I can start the winter quarter."*
"Well Mrs. Carlton said she'll help you with everything including the financial aid, so why don't you call her," Lisa looking at clothes.
"I want to do this on my own, pay my own way," Lee pushes the cart.
"$647 is a lot of money and that not counting book," Lisa told her.
"Well, I have been saving so I should be able to pay. Besides, it means a lot to me if I do it."
"Why," Lisa paused to look at Lee.
"Up until now, I had to depend on others like you and Kelly. Now I can take care of myself. I don't want to depend on anyone else. My father taught me, anything worth having is worth working for. I want to show I can do this."
"You don't have to show me anything, baby, I know you can."
"Still, I have to show me though."

103

Lee stopped in the game section and looked at the different selections and prices.

"Is this really important to you," Lisa walked up behind Lee.
"Yeah, it is," Lee looked at Lisa, seeking her approval.
"Then I'll support any decision you make."
"Thanks," Lee said happily like a little kid, she hugged Lisa.

Lee and Lisa continued shopping. Lisa picked out some clothes, boxers, socks and shoes for Lee and Quincy and an X-BOX with games. Lee bought an ankle bracelet and 24 carets gold ring with Lisa initials engraved inside the band and a bath set and for Quincy a football and bike. They also buy stuff for the house. Lisa offers to help pick out gifts for Renee and Simon.

As they head to the check out line, Lee spots a Florida Jersey with matching hat. She recalls Kelly talking about how she wanted to live there. Lee got if for her.

"I think she'll like it," Lee said to Lisa.
"I know she will."

After checking out, Lee pushed the cart to the vehicle and helped load the gifts inside. On the way home, they stopped at a lot selling Christmas trees. Walking around, they spotted the tree they want and pay for it. With help from the employees, Lee tied the tree to the top of the vehicle and her and Lisa head home.

"Now I can have the Christmas I always wanted," Lee said.

Lee leaned her head back and looked out the window for the drive home.

Chapter Sixteen

With Christmas only a few days away, the Bailey household was busy. Christmas music was playing on the radio and Lisa was fixing her Christmas dinner; turkey, stuffing, stuff cabbage, yams, macaroni and cheese and greens and for dessert a German chocolate cake.

Lee and Quincy were decorating the tree with lights, tinsels and colorful bulbs. Lee helps Quincy place the star at the top of the tree. The outside of the house had flashing lights strung up across the porch. A snowman sat in the front yard and a Christmas wreath hangs on the door.

A little later in the evening, Lee helped Lisa wraps gift. Lee told her she talked to Renee about going to school.

"So what she said?" Lisa put a bow on a gift.
"She said she was happy for me and if I needed her for anything to call."
"You tell her you're paying for the tuition," Lisa looked at Lee.
"Yes."
"And."
"She said if that's what I want to do, then ok, that she understand my reason."

A few seconds later, Quincy came into the living room excited.

"Mommy, Lee, look, it's snowing outside."

They both go to the door and look out. Snow was coming down slowly, turning the yard into a winter wonderland. As it fell, Lee couldn't help but feel like a kid inside. It had been awhile since she last had a snowy Christmas.

She was a child and her father was still alive. After the first snow fell, he would take her to the park and they would go down the hill on sleds. They would make snow angels and have snowball fights. They would make snow castles and the biggest snowman. When it got dark, Lee and her father would head home, she up on his board shoulders as he carried the sleighs. Once home, they would have hot chocolate and make smores in the fire place and listen to Christmas music on the radio. He would sing to her, sometimes she would joining in with him.

Always before bed as he would tuck her in. Lee's father would tell the story of the birth of Jesus. He tell her; *"God gift to us was his son, that's how much he loved us. Always have a good heart, even when it's hard to. In the end it will pay off."*

He would kiss her goodnight and said *"I love you angel."*

"Listen mommy," Quincy said as he turned up the radio.

"I'm dreaming of a white Christmas…
Just like the one I use to know…"

As Lee and Quincy listen to Bing Crosby sing "White Christmas," Lisa went into the kitchen to fix some hot chocolate for everyone. She came back into the living room and sat on the couch with Lee as Quincy sat on the floor.

As the song played, Lee remembered her Christmas with her father and how much fun she had with him, even when he got sick. Christmas for her was sharing it with him.

As Bing Crosby continued to sing, everyone looked out the window and enjoyed the moment.

Chapter Seventeen

Christmas morning! As Lisa went into the kitchen to fix breakfast, Lee put on her jacket and shoes and headed outside. The snow last night as accumulated and hadn't been walked on.

Lee fell on the ground and began to make snow angels. Quincy who came out his room saw Lee and joined her. Lisa stood in the doorway and looked on.

Lisa shook her head and laughed as Lee and her son had a snowball fight. Lisa smiled as she heard them laughing and having fun running around hitting each other with snowballs. She knew this meant a lot to Lee and let her enjoyed herself.

Fifteen minutes later, Lee and Quincy come inside and went into their room to take off their wet clothes and changed into dried ones. When they finished, they entered into the kitchen as Lisa finished cooking breakfast: Pancakes, sausage, eggs and grits.

After breakfast, Quincy cleared the table and Lee helped Lisa with the dishes. Once the kitchen was clean, everyone headed into the living room to open their gifts.

"Thanks mommy," Quincy opened his gift, *"Thanks Lee."*

Lee opened her next gift and smiled, *"Thanks babe,"* she hugged Lisa.

Lisa opened her gift, *"This is nice."*

Lee bought her an ankle bracelet.

"I have one more gift," Lee said.

Hurrying into the bedroom, Lee came back out carrying a large box.

"What's that," Lisa looked at Lee suspicious.
"Open it," Lee looked at Quincy who smiling.
"Yeah mommy, open it."
"What did you do, Lee?" Lisa still looking at her.
"Will you just open it," Lee pleaded.

Lisa opened the box and let out a high gasp.

"Oh...my...God..." I can't believe it.

Lisa pulled out the coat she seen at Macy's.

"You didn't, I told you..."
"I know what you told me but I just couldn't help it. I went down to the store and talk to the manager. I explained to him the situation and asked if he could help me out."
"How much did you pay?"
"1500, feel inside the pocket," Lee said still smiling.

Lisa felt inside the pocket and pulled out a small box. She looked at Lee and her son who are both sitting there looking like two kids who are up to no good. When Lisa opened the box she cried out.

"Baby, it's beautiful. This is too much," Lee said wiping back tears.
"I wanted you to have it, you deserve it," Lee put the ring on Lisa finger.
"Mommy, you like your gift?"
"Yes dear, I do."
"I love you," Lee said.

"I love you too," Lisa kissed Lee.

After getting dressed in the outfit Lisa brought her, she Lisa in blue jeans, Michigan sweater and Nike's and Quincy in grey slacks, grey shirt headed out the house. They made a stop at Kelly's apartment and went up to see her.

"Merry Christmas," Lee said as they entered the apartment.

Lisa, Lee and Quincy took a seat as Lee handed Kelly her gift. Kelly opened it and smiled.

"Thanks dawg," Kelly hugged Lee.
"Don't mention it," Lee said.
"Tonight you're welcome to our house for dinner." Lisa said to Kelly.
"I'm ok," Kelly put on her hat.
"You don't have to spend Christmas alone," Lee looked at her.
"Who said I'm alone."
"Well, if you change your mind," Lisa said.
"I'm ok, don't worry about me, enjoy today with your family."

Lee grabbed Kelly hand and pulled her into a half hug.

"You know I'm here, were here for you."
"I know, I know, now go, enjoy."

They leave the apartment and headed out to the car. Lisa drove off.

"You know she lied about being by herself." Lisa said to Lee.
"I know but Kelly got to much pride to admit that."

"Well, we tried. Lisa said.

Back at the house, Lee got ready for her sister and the rest of her family to come over for dinner. A half-hour later, the doorbell rang and Lee opened the door. Inside everyone took a seat as everyone exchanged gifts.

"I hope you like them," Lee said to Renee and Simon. *"Lisa help me pick them out."*

Lee handed Renee a gold necklace with a cross on it and gave Simon a hand held baseball game.

"There nice, thank you." Renee and Simon said.

Lisa pulled out two gift certificates and handed them to Aunt Fannie and Keshia.

"We didn't know what to get, so we got you these gift certificates to Bath and Body."
"Thank you," Aunt Fannie said.

Renee and Aunt Fannie handed Lee and Lisa their gifts: from her and Simon, bedroom and bath items and from Auntie and Keshia, gift certificates and a game for Quincy. Renee also gave her sister a journal to write her thoughts in and a book by *Maya Angelou.*

"Who this young man?" Renee noticed Quincy.
"This is my son, Quincy."
"Nice to meet you," Renee shook his hand.
"Hi," he said shyly.
"Quincy, this is my sister and her son Simon." Lee introduced them.

Quincy said hi to Simon.

"Mommy can we go play my game?" Quincy asked Lisa.

"If it's ok with Ms. Renee," Lisa looked at Renee.

Renee nodded her head and him and Simon went into his room.

Everyone sat, talked, sung and exchanged stories about their favorite Christmas. Renee remembered her and her mom the night before, decorating and singing carols. Auntie and Keisha would come over for a big dinner. Later on that night they went Christmas caroling. They would go home and exchange gifts. The next morning, they go to shelters and serve food then to hospitals to visit the sick.

"Sound like you guys had fun." Lee said.
"We did child," Aunt Fannie said. *"Your mom would sing this solo that would take your breath away."*
"Mom, sing the song Aunt Leigh would sing," Keshia said.
"Yeah mommy, sing," Simon said, who came out the room with Quincy.

Aunt Fannie:
Lord thank you for loving me...
My soul does magnify your name...
Even when my steps get hard and I can't see my way...
You came along and carry me, guide me, help me along
my way...
My soul loves you Lord...
You're my rock, my sword my shield...
No other help I know...
Thank you, thank you my God...
My soul does magnify your name"

Renee:
Lord thank you for loving me…
My soul does magnify your name…
Even when storm clouds rolls and the sun doesn't
shine…
You came along and carry me, guide me, help me along
my way…
My soul loves you Lord…
You're my rock, my sword, my shield…
No other help I know…
Thank you, thank you my God…
My soul does magnify your name"

Aunt Fannie and Renee:
Even when temptations arise and I stumble and fall…
You came along and carry me, guide me and help me…
Along my way, each and every day…
My soul loves you Lord…
You're my rock (Aunt Fannie), *my sword* (Renee)….
My shield (unison)….
No other help I know…
Thank you, thank you my God…
For my soul do magnify your name (Renee).

"That was beautiful," Lisa said clapping her hands.

All Lee could say was *wow* as the others clapped their hands too.

"I hope I wasn't off beat," Renee said.
"No, no, that was nice." Lee commented.
"Auntie, sing ma ma favorite Christmas song." Simon said.
"Child, I'm tired." Aunt Fannie caught her breath.
"Please," Simon pleaded.
"Go head mom," Keshia said.

"Mind as well, auntie," Renee smiled at her aunt.

Aunt Fannie started humming softly. With a low voice, she started singing "Silent Night." With every note, there was power behind the words. Aunt Fannie swayed back and forth, her eyes closed. As she sung, Aunt Fannie made you feel the song, believe in the song, as if you were there the night Jesus was born. When she was done singing, everyone was quite.

"I'm speechless. I don't know what to say," Lee said.
"That was lovely," Lisa add.
"Thank you," Aunt Fannie replied. *"Your mom and I would sing in the church choir. She would do solos that brought joy to your soul and tears to your eyes. Whatever you came in with bothering you, you left church feeling hope. My sister would say, "There is nothing too hard for my God to fix." She said that in spite of her circumstances, God is still God. Your mom loved to sing, it made her feel good inside. Singing was what made her happy the most. That and the love for her family."*

Lee sat and listened to more stories about her mom as everyone made their way into the dining room for the Christmas dinner. After Aunt Fannie said grace, everyone ate, talked, laugh and sang of good cheer.

Chapter Eighteen

Lee and Lisa were out shopping for clothes for the New Year Eve's party at the club. After shopping, Lisa drove over to Kelly's apartment so Lee could see how she was doing.

After pulling up to park, Lee and Lisa heard voices coming from Kelly's apartment. Looking up they saw Kelly and Alexis coming outside arguing on the steps. Lee noticed a younger man standing off in the shadows looking hard at Kelly but she didn't pay him any attention.

Getting out the car, Lee walked up to Kelly and Alexis to see what's up.

"Kel, what's up," she asked stepping between them.
"This bitch!" Kelly yells.
"What happen?" Lee looked at Alexis who was crying.
"I'm tired of your shit," Alexis yells back. *"You said you want to work things out and to come home, and what I do, I come back and see you fucking some other bitch, fuck you Kelly!"*
"You should have called before you came," Kelly said with a smirk on her face. *"That's on you."*

Alexis slapped Kelly hard in the face. Shocked, Kelly went to hit Alexis.

"Dawg, no!" Lee stopped her.
"I'm tired of you disrespecting me; I'm tired of the abuse, the cheating, and the lies. You don't know what the hell you want. I'm done Kelly, you can go to hell!" Alexis said with her body trembling with rage.

Alexis tried to hit Kelly again but Kelly grabbed her and pushed her against the building. Lee stepped in, and shoved Kelly back.

> *"Kel, chill! It's over!* Lisa pushed her back.
> *"Bitch, fuck you!"* Kelly spits.
> *"No, fuck you!"*

Alexis reached around Lee and slapped Kelly again, scratching her face.

> *"Bitch,"* Kelly grabbed her face. *"I'll fuck you up!"*

Kelly lunged at her but Lee stopped her again.

> *"I'm tired of your shit. I stuck by you, tried to love you. I gave you everything, I gave you my all,"* Alexis shouted. *"You don't want that though, you don't want anything better for yourself!"*

Alexis was hurt. Tears streamed down her face.

> *"Whatever bitch!"* Kelly smiled at Alexis, rubbing her hand over the scratch marks.
> *"I got your bitch."*

Kelly made one last effort to get at Alexis but Lee stopped her. Kelly told Lee to move but Lee didn't budge. Lee desperately tried to get her to calm down.

> *"I'm through,"* Alexis said wiping the tears away. *"No more. Fuck whoever you want to, that's what you're going to do anyway."*
> *"I don't need you,"* Kelly smirked. *"You want to leave, then leave, hoe."*

"Kel, calm the fuck down." Lee pleaded pushing her up against the building.

Lee turned to Alexis.

"Go on Alexis, leave."
"She'll never be happy. Lee, she wants to be miserable, she wants everyone around her to be miserable with her." Alexis said to Lee.
"Lee, just let Kelly go!" Lisa said watching from the car. *"Kelly going to do whatever the fuck she wants to do."*
"Kel, let her go, it's over, just let her leave." Lee begged as she'd restrained her.

Lee turned for a split second and watched Alexis walk away. As she watched, Lee again noticed the young man in the same spot. This time, Lee paid attention.

She noticed a bulge in the man jacket. When he unzipped his jacket, Lee saw a gun. It didn't register yet that something might be wrong. Lisa also saw the gun, she quickly got out the car and headed towards Lee.

Kelly took this opportunity and came around Lee and walked toward Alexis who was walking back to the apartment. Alexis stopped in her tracks, her face frozen with fear. Alexis turned around and looked at Kelly then Lee.

Lee who saw Alexis's face and saw Lisa get out the car. Suddenly Lee had in eerie feeling overcome her. Quickly walking to Kelly who was close to the steps. Lee tried to stop her. Lee broke into a run as Kelly reached the steps. Kelly didn't notice the man. Her attention was set on Alexis who was blocking her view.

"Kelly, stop!" Lee yelled still running.

Kelly turned back, looked at Lee and waved her off. She turned around and faces Alexis who's terrified.

"Baby, wait," Kelly said sarcastically.
"Are you Kelly Peters," a voice asked.
"Yeah, who wants to know?"

The young man steps from out of the shadows.

"Who the fuck is you?"

The man pulled out a gun and points it at Kelly. Kelly looked at the gun, then at the man, smirked.

"And," throwing her hands in the air in a nonchalant way.

Pop! Pop! Pop! Pop!

Kelly stumbled back and fell to one knee. Alexis screamed, *"No!"*

Lisa saw Lee running and yells *"Lee stop!"*

Lee didn't stop, reaching Kelly as she collapsed into her arms. Kelly had been shot twice in the chest and once in the abdomen and arm. Lee held her friend as tears streamed down her face.

Kelly eyes were opened. Her breathing became shallow and labored. Blood was coming out of her mouth as she tried to talk.

"Someone call 911!" Lee yelled trying to stop the bleeding.

Alexis and Lisa reached them, Alexis hysterical.

"Hold on dawg," Lee told Kelly, fighting back tears. *"Hold on."*

Kelly coughed and blood splatters on Lee's shirt. People started to gather at the scene, whispering among themselves, shaking their head at what just happened.

"The police are on the way!" A woman yelled from the crowd.

Kelly shirt was soaked with blood as she blead faster. Her chest starting to rise and fall slowly.

"Hold on Kel, you're going to make it, everything going to be alright." Lee said.
"Promise me..." Kelly tried to sit up.
"Don't talk," Lee said. *"The squad is almost here."*

Sirens heard in the background became closer.

"You're gonna get fix soon. You'll be back to yourself being an ass hole," Lee said with a half smile.

Kelly tried to smile as she shook her head.

"No, listen. Promise me," Kelly whispered as she grabbed Lee's shirt and pulled her closer.
"Anything, you name it."
"Promise, me, you'll never, change, who, you, are..."
"I promise, now you just hang in there, ok."

Kelly laughed. She cough up more blood.

"I need you, Kelly, you got to fight to live," Lee cried.

Sirens sound louder as the squad became closer.

"You can't leave me, Kel, fight!"

Kelly shook her head no. She took her finally breath and died. Lee shook her, crying harder.

"Kel, Kel, don't die on me, I need you! Kelly, please!"

Lisa was crying as she held Alexis in her arms. Alexis cried too. Lee put her head into Kelly's chest and cried uncontrollably.

"No! No! No" Lee screamed *"God no!"*

Chapter Nineteen

Lee sat on the steps near where Kelly died. She was in shock, as tears streamed down her face. Lee held Kelly's bloody shirt in her hands, staring down at the ground.

The police sealed off the scene with yellow tape. Detectives interviewed people, asking them what they seen and heard.

Alexis stood with Lisa. Alexis talked to the lead detective and tried giving a description of the man. She broke down mid-way through.

"Officer, please escort this lady," the detective pointed at Alexis. *"Take her to the cruiser and see if she needs anything."*

A female officer came and helped Alexis to the cruiser, with Lisa on the other side.

Renee and Aunt Fannie showed up. At first they saw Kelly's body on the ground covered up and thinks it's Lee.

"No!" Renee screamed as she tried to cross the tape. A police officer stopped her.
"Officer, please, I need to get through," Renee pleaded.
"Ma'me, I'm sorry but this is a crime scene. I can't let you through."
"Please," Renee begged.

Lisa looked up and saw Renee and Aunt Fannie standing behind the yellow tape, trying to get through.
She told a detective standing near who they were and he let them pass.

Renee and Aunt Fannie rushed over to Lisa. When they get there, Renee asked if it was Lee. Lisa said no and pointed to her sitting on the steps.

"If it's not her, then who"... Aunt Fannie asked.
"Kelly," Lisa answered sadly.
"Dear Jesus," Aunt Fannie, said clutching her chest.

Renee looked over to her sister and whispered, *"All sis."* Renee walked over to her and placed her hand on her shoulder.

"Sis, I'm so sorry," she whispered. *"I know she meant a lot to you."*

Lee didn't say anything. She looked as the corner put Kelly's in a body bag and loaded her into the coroner's van. As the van pulled off, Lee dropped her head and cried.

"Lee," Renee kneeled down and hugged her sister.

Lisa and Aunt Fannie come over. Everyone felt helpless, not knowing how to comfort Lee.

"Does she have any family that needs to be contacted?" Aunt Fannie asked.
"Kelly had a grandmother who raised her but their relationship is strange." Lisa said, wiping her face.
"What about her mother or father?" Renee asked.
"Her mom is an addict, her father, she never knew."
"That poor child, to die alone." Aunt Fannie shook her head.
"She didn't die alone," Lee stood up. *"She had me."*
"Sis, auntie didn't mean..."
"My best friend, died in my arms, right here," Lee pointed to the spot where her body was.

"Baby," Lisa walked over to her.

"Where Alexis?" Lee asked, looking around.

"She's with the police." Lisa said.

"I got to go." Lee rubbed her hair and face.

"Go where." Renee asked, slightly worried.

"I don't know, I just got to get away from here."

"I'm coming." Lisa said.

"No, you stay with Alexis and make sure she's alright. I just need time to myself."

"But Lee," Lisa interjected but Lee stopped her.

Lee walked over to Alexis and hugged her, telling her she was there for her. Lee then turned and walked down the street as Lisa, Renee and Aunt Fannie helplessly watched.

Chapter Twenty

Lee sat on the bottom monkey bars at the abandoned school. She remembered back to how she and Kelly would come here to drink and talk until the sun came up. How Kelly was there when her dad died. She remembered how Kelly would stand up for her when the other girls would bully her. How Kelly would tease her on how she talked or how her laugh sounded. Lee remembered the last thing Kelly said to her;

"Promise me you'll never change who you are."
"I promise."

Lee remembered how Kelly looked when she took her last breath. Kelly went out like she said she would; unafraid. Still clinging to the bloody shirt, she broke down.

After sitting for a half-hour, Lee got up and walked over to a trash can. Putting the shirt inside. Lee poured liquor inside and set the shirt on fire. Standing there, Lee watched the fire burn, tears streaming down her face.

Lee left the school yard and walked around. Her mind wondering. As people passed by, Lee didn't notice them. It was bad if she was the only person out.

An hour later, Lee came up to an old red and white barn style house. She walked up the gravel walkway to the front porch. An engraving going across the mailbox read, "The Peters Family." Kelly's grandmother home. Lee knocked on the door and waited. A few seconds later an older white lady with a cane came to the door.

"Yes, may I help you?" The woman asked through the screen door.
"Hi, Mrs. Peters, I'm Lee, Kelly friend."

"Yes," she said through the screen.

"I thought," Lee said choking back tears. *"I thought you want to know that earlier today, Kelly was shot and killed."*

"Kelly made her choice on how she wanted to live her life. Now if you excuse me."

As Mrs. Peter went to close the front door, Lee opened the screen door and blocked the door open.

"Don't you care that your granddaughter was killed." Lee said upset.

"I stop caring about what Kelly did years ago, now if you please get off my porch."

Mrs. Peters still tried to close the door but Lee stopped her.

"Young lady please, if you don't leave, I'll call the police."

Kelly was your flesh and blood, how you not care?"

Kelly made the choice to leave, just like her mother, all she had to do..."

"What, do as you say, become what you wanted?"

"The Bible said..."

"No disrespect, I don't care. Everybody interprets what they think the Bible means. No one really understand it though, not truly."

Lee shook her head and sighed.

"Yes Kelly lived her life, not yours. Since when did that become a sin? All you ever did was judge Kelly, looked down on her, condemning her to hell. In your eyes, she was never good enough."

"She was a sinner."

"Yeah, we all are, but God forgave. Why can't you."

Mrs. Peters didn't say anything, she just looked at Lee.

"Look, Kelly wasn't perfect. She made mistakes, we all do, but she was my best friend. She lived how she wanted to. I can't judge Kelly, no one can. I just hope now that the peace she was longing for, she finally had. My father always told me the only thing that is required of you here in life is that you try and do right and that in the end when you stand before God, only him do you account to, only He can judge us, not man."

Lee stepped back out the door, closing the screen door. As she headed down the steps, she stopped and turned around.

"Like I said, I thought you might want to know Kelly died but I guess I was wrong."

Lee turned and continued down the stairs. Mrs. Peters stood in the doorway as tears fell from her eyes watch as Lee walked down the street.

It's late when Lee finally arrived home. Going into the house, Lisa was in the living room waiting for her.

Lee sat down next to her and placed her head into Lisa lap. Lisa stroked Lee's hair as Lee closed her eyes. Images of the final moments, the gun shot, Kelly falling, Kelly taking her last breath, played in her head as she let the tears fall. Lisa leaned down and whispered into Lee's ear that she sorry gently kissed her on the forehead. Lee cried harder as Lisa desperately tried to console her. With tears also streaming down her face, Lisa held Lee as Lee cried herself to sleep in her arms.

Chapter Twenty-One

It had been one week since Kelly death. Lee kept herself busy by working. Renee and Lisa thought it was too soon for her to go back to work. Mrs. Carlton offered to talk to her boss considering the circumstance. Lee didn't want to sit around and think about what happened to her friend.

Lee time consisted of going to work and to the school yard. She stayed there until it got late then just walked around before going home.

Lee didn't sleep at night, staying up watching TV all night or sitting on the front porch. When she did try to sleep, she tossed and turned. Haunted by the images of Kelly's death.

Lee went through the motions of living. She knew she had to go on but didn't know how. Her best friend since childhood, her "sister," shot down in front of her.

As Lee sat and stared out into the world, Lisa watched from a distance, worried that Lee would snap at any time.

One day, after Lisa came home from work, she saw Lee sitting on the porch swinging. Lisa sat down beside her and held her hand.

"Alexis called the other day." Lisa said.
"How she doing?"
"She still hurting but she's holding up. The funeral is tomorrow. She said the police told her, the guy that shot Kelly had some kind of beef with her."
"What kind of beef?"
"Apparently, the guy sister, Kelly was not only messing with, but also got her hooked on crack. The girl OD last week on crack and died. It seemed like she had a future."

Lee sat quietly.

"Baby, I know you don't want to hear this but Kelly brought all this on herself."
"I don't give a fuck," jumped up. *"She didn't have to die like a dog in the streets! He had a problem with her; he should have came to her face up, not hiding behind the shadows."*

Lee stormed into the house, Lisa was behind her.

"Lee, Kelly did as she wanted but what she did affected everybody else. Somebody died because of her actions."
"So, what, she had to die?"
"I didn't say that." Lisa tried to sound empathic reaching for Lee hand.

Lee headed into the kitchen and poured herself a glass of water. Standing at the sink, she drunk it. Lisa walked in and took a seat. She looked at Lee.

"Your sister and aunt are worried about you, and frankly, so am I."
"Why, don't be, I'll be fine."

Lee put her glass into the sink.

Getting up, *"Baby, please don't shut me out."*

Lisa walked up to Lee and placed her hand on the side of Lee's face. Lee just looked at her.

"Did the police catch the guy?" Lee asked.
"There still looking for him."
"He'll get his," Lee mumbled, turning away.

Lisa turned Lee around, *"What that supposes to mean?"*
"Like, I said, he'll get his, one way or the other."
Lisa grabbed her arm, *"Lee don't do anything stupid."*
"My best friend died in my arms," Lee hit her chest.
"Don't you get that!" Lee yelled.

Turning back to the sink, Lee picked up the glass and threw it across the room toward the wall, shattering it.

"Killing that man not going to bring Kelly back!" Lisa yelled back, tears starting to fall.

Lisa reached for Lee but Lee jerked back.

"Baby. I know you're hurting and it hurts me that I can't make this pain go away. Kelly was your best friend and even though I didn't agree with what she did, I understand she meant a lot to you, and you loved her. But the fact still remains, no matter what, Kelly died from how she lived her life and nothing you do or say is going to change that."

Lee tried to walk away but Lisa stopped her.

"Are you listening? Going out there and doing something to that man, is not the answer." Lisa stroked Lee's face and wiped away the tears as they fell, *"If you kill him, you're no better than him. You're not Kelly. You owe her nothing, not your life, not your freedom! This is not your fight!"*
"I don't care!"

Lee jerked from Lisa's grip and walked out the kitchen.

"Baby, your better than this. Why are you going to throw everything away, for what?"

"She was my best friend!" Lee turned and yelled at Lisa.

Lisa stood there not knowing what to do or what was going to happen next. She watched as Lee body shook with rage and anger. Hurt that she couldn't do anything to help Lee.

Lee turned and walked out the door and left the house.

"Lee wait! Where are you going?" Lisa said walking to her.

"I don't know."

"Baby, please don't go." Lisa pleaded, worried at what Lee might do.

Lee didn't listen, rather didn't care. She shook her head and stepped back from Lisa and walked off the porch and down the street. Lisa upset and concern, went on into the house and called Renee.

"Hello, Renee…hi…I'm sorry to call you so late but I'm worried about Lee…"

Lisa proceeded to tell Renee what happened at the house and that Lee left without saying where she was going. Lisa told her she was also afraid at what Lee might do.

Chapter Twenty-Two

It was three a.m. and there was a knock at Renee's door. Renee opened the door and let Lee in.

Lee didn't say anything as she sat down in the chair. Renee asked if she liked anything and Lee said no. Sitting on the couch, Renee waited for her sister to speak.

"Did Lisa call you?" Lee asked, looking up.
"Yes, she was worried about you, frankly we all are."
"No need to be."
"Why."
"I'll be fine."
"According to Lisa, you're not fine, and I have to agree with her, sitting here looking at you carry the weight of the world on your shoulders."
"Well, there no need to be."
"Well I'm sorry, I disagree. Sis, all we want to do is be here for you, but you won't let us. Me, auntie and Lisa, let us help you through this."

Lee got up and went over to the mantel and stared at the pictures of her mom. Renee looked on, her heart ached at not knowing how to fix this for her sister.

"What do you think mom would say?"
Getting up, Renee walked over to her, *"She would say, she understand you lost a friend but won't pretend to know how you feel. She would tell you that in time the healing will begin, and never to forget the good times you two shared and to always keep her close in your heart."*

Renee stood near Lee at the mantel. She reached out and put her hand on her shoulder.

"Is that what you believed when mom died?"

"Yes, I had to. If I hadn't, mom death would have made me bitter. Her death would have destroyed me inside."

Renee turned Lee around to face her, *"Sis, I can't begin to imagine how you feel right now and I won't try to. To do so would be an insult to you. But I will tell you this, when I got to the scene and seen the body lying there and I thought it was you, I became scared. I felt God was playing some kind of cruel joke on me. Bringing you back into my life, just to take you away tragically."*

Renee looked at Lee, looking for some sign that she was listening to what she was saying.

"Like I told you, the only thing I care about is you and your happiness. Lee, Lisa told me you were thinking about going after that man. She also talked to me about who Kelly was. That's not going to bring her back; all it's going to do is make a bad situation worse. Violence never solved anything. You don't believe me, call auntie, she'll tell you the same thing, she was worried about you too. Lisa is right too about Kelly, Kelly lived her life the way she knew how, it's time to live your own."

Lee let tears fell as Renee hugged her.

"We are here for you. Don't lock us out; let us help you through this."

The next morning Lee woke up on Renee's couch. Today was Kelly funeral. Sitting there, Lee tried to come to grips over the fact the she would never see her best friend again.

Lee got up and went into the bathroom. She turned on the water at the sink, splashed the water on her face and looked at herself in the mirror. How could she go on without her friend in her life? Renee was right though, she had to live her life and not anyone else.

Splashing water on her face again, Lee turned off the faucets and dried her hands and face on a hand towel lying on the sink.

Lee went into the kitchen and was surprised to see Lisa sitting at the table. Lisa got up and walked over to Lee, and hugged her.

"Are you ok?" Lisa asked.

Lee nodded yes as Lisa gently squeezed her hand. Sitting back down, Renee served breakfast.

"I called Lisa last night and told her you were ok and would be staying the night."
"Thanks." Lee said softly.
"The police caught the man who shot Kelly."

Renee handed Lee the morning paper. On the front page was a caption of the man arrested for killing Kelly.

"That's good." Lisa looked at Lee.

Lee sat and read the article.

"I bought you a change of clothes for the funeral."
"Thanks. How Alexis?" Lee asked playing with her food.
"Still having a hard time dealing with this but she said she'll be at the service."
"Sis, you should eat something." Renee said.
"I'm not really hungry, excuse me."

Lee got up from the table and took the clothes and went into the bathroom to get dress. Lee had a hard time as she took a shower, playing over in her head the shooting. Lee let the water run down her body as a sick feeling overwhelmed her.

After her shower, Lee took her time getting dress, trying to fight back tears. Sitting on the edge of the bathtub, Lee composed herself, feeling of rage and anger built up inside. Getting up she looked into the mirror.

"I promise, Kelly." She whispered.

Lee headed out the bathroom and into the living room where Renee and Lisa are waiting.

"I know I didn't know her but I would like to go and pay my respect, if you don't mind."

Lee smiled and said yes. Lisa looked at her and gave her reassurance that everything will be alright.

"Your aunt called and said she'll meet us at the funeral home." Lisa adjusted Lee's collar.

Lee nodded and soon everybody headed out to the funeral home for Kelly service.

The service for Kelly Angel Peters was nice. People who knew Kelly sent flowers and cards; former teachers, people she ran with in the streets, even her former parole officer sent a condolence card saying the Kelly had potential and sad that she never knew it.

Kelly was buried in the outfit Lee bought her for Christmas. Alexis insisted on her wearing it. Kelly was even wearing her glasses, something she never did in public. Kelly felt like a nerd when she put them on even though she was book smart as well as street smart. In all honesty Kelly could have been anything she wanted, if she gave herself a chance. But circumstances took those chances away, and as far as Kelly was concerned she wasn't worth it to anyone or herself. She never learned how to believe. She felt she didn't have a right to.

Not a lot of people in at the funeral home. Lee was there with Lisa, Renee, Alexis and Aunt Fannie. A couple of other people that use to hang out with her were there. Some people Lee didn't recognize. Lee looked around for Kelly grandmother but wasn't surprise not to see her.

"I'm surprise she didn't show." Renee whispered down to Lee.
"I'm not."

Lee took her seat next to Lisa as service started. An older lady began to sing "Precious Lord."

"Precious Lord,
Take my hand, lead me on help me stand
I am tired, I am weak, and I am worn
Through the storm, through the night,
Lead me on to the light
Take my hand, Precious Lord and lead me home…"

Lee tried to hold back tears as the woman sung. Putting her head into her hands, Lee couldn't help but cry. Lisa rubbed her back, comforting her.

"When my way grows drear
Precious Lord lingers near
When my light is almost gone
Hear my cry, hear my call

Hold my hand lest I fall
Take my hand, Precious Lord and lead me home…"

Lisa began crying as she tried to console Alexis who completely broke down. Even Aunt Fannie shed a tear for a senseless loss. Renee got up and went on the other side of her sister. Renee held her as Lee cried into her arms.

"When darkness appears and the night draws near
And the day is past gone
At the river I stand
Guide my feet, hold my hand
Take my hand, Precious Lord and lead me home…"

The minister talked about violence among young people and taking the streets back. He talked about tough love and more parenting and guidance. He spoke about getting involved in the church doing more so another young child didn't lose his or her life.

Before the service ended, the minister asked if anyone would like to say a few words on Kelly behalf.

Lisa looked at Lee and told her to go up. Lee looked at Renee who smiled and nodded her head. Lee got up and slowly walked to the front. As she passed the casket, she looked and saw Kelly lying peacefully. Grabbing hold of the mic, Lee cleared her throat and softly spoke.

"Hi, I'm Lee; Kelly was, um, my best friend. Kelly was… Kelly, she did as she liked and didn't care if someone liked it or not."

Lee struggled to find the strength to keep on.

"Kelly wasn't perfect. She had her faults but she was my best friend that I would be missed. She taught me to be myself and not change for anyone. She made me promise that before she, um died." Tears flowed. *"She taught me to not please anyone because they will still be who they are in the end. Kelly taught me how to be independent, strong and how to have patients,* (chuckles), *like she had room to talk. One day, Kelly told me I was lucky because I had a family who loved me.*

Kelly died in my arms that day. I'll never forget her," Lee looked up. *"I love you dawg."*

Lee finished and walked back to her seat. She looked up and saw Kelly's grandmother sitting in the back row. Tears streamed down her face. Taking her seat, Lisa put her arm around her as Lee placed her head in Lisa chest and cried softly.

Chapter Twenty-Three

A New Year! It had been two weeks since Kelly funeral. This was the first year that Lee brought it in without her best friend. Lee kept her feelings inside, not talking to anyone about Kelly.

Lee went on with her life, throwing herself into her work. She registered classes for winter quarter to Lisa and Renee relief. Going to school helped Lee out. Her writing class was her outlet for what she was unable to communicate.

Lee was doing well in her two classes. In journalism she had a B average and in creative writing, she maintained a C average. Her instructors encourage her, offering constructive criticism. They tell her that she had a good gift that she could improve on.

"You have something special inside," one said.
"Don't be afraid to show others what you can do, believe in yourself," another said.

During her breaks and lunches and on weekends, Lee worked on her writing. Writing on just about anything special to her father, mother, her sister, Kelly, and herself. Lee tapped into her deepest feelings and express them on paper. For her, this was easy. This way she could let people know who she was and how she felt without struggling with the words.

"This is good," Renee said reading one of her sister papers. *"You have a lot to say."*
"Thank you."

Lee was sitting in the kitchen with Renee. She came by to show her a writing assignment she was doing for class.

"You think about writing professionally?"

"No," Lee shrugged.

"Why not?"

"I don't know. I do this for fun. Besides I don't think I'm that good."

"Sis, but you are good, even your teachers think so."

"I don't see myself smart though."

"Well you are. You got talent. You're able to do what came natural to you. Some people can't. You should give yourself a chance."

"I still don't know."

"Believe in yourself. I do and I know Lisa does too."

"She does," Lee smiled. *"She said if I try hard enough, I can be anything I want."*

"So what's stopping you?"

"I guess nothing really."

"Exactly, hits the table with her fingers, *At least try, for me."*

Renee got up and went to the desk drawer. Looking through it, she pulled out a piece of paper. Sitting back down, she handed the paper to Lee who looked at it.

"It's a contest for people who like to write. When you told me you were going to college for creative writing, I thought about you. I pulled it off the internet."

"I'm not sure," Lee hesitant.

"Just give it a chance," Renee smiled. *"You might like it."*

Lee agreed she will.

"So how is Alexis doing?" Renee sipped her coffee.

"I really haven't seen her since the funeral. I talked with her briefly on the phone. She said she's trying to hold up but it's hard."

"I bet she misses Kelly."

"She does. She said it's hard for her to stay at the apartment with Kelly things there and the memories. So she going to pack up her things and send some to her grandmother and the rest she'll give to me."

"What is she going to do now that Kelly is gone?"

"She said she might move back to New York with her mom and sister."

"Well, I hope everything works out for her."

"Yeah, I hope so too."

"And how are you holding up?" Renee looked at Lee.

"It's hard, I admit. I don't have my friend here to talk to, to laugh with."

"Is writing helping you some?"

"Yeah, feelings that I have trouble expressing, I can write down."

"That's good. How does Lisa feel about all of this?"

"Ok, I guess. Since Kelly died, Lisa gave me my space to figure out and deal with what happen that day."

"That good," Renee nodded.

"Lisa good like that, she said not being able to help me was the hardest for her."

"Well, sounds like she really cares about you."

"She does."

"Well any time you want to talk, I'm here for you."

"Thanks."

As time went on, Lee continued to work and went to school. She tried not to lose focus on what it is she was trying to accomplish in life for herself.

It was hard and at times she struggled. Getting frustrated, sometimes wanting to quit. When she had her down time, she thought about Kelly and the last time she saw her, hurting that she will never see her again. Lee kept going though; she knew Kelly would want her to.

"Just because my life ended doesn't mean yours have to either. Do you, be you, never stop," she heard Kelly's voice.

Lee showed Lisa the paper. Renee gave her compliments on the writing contest.

"Are you going to enter?" Lisa asked as she set the table for dinner.
"I don't know, Renee thinks I should."
"I think you should too, your good. I hear you at night in the room talking to yourself as you write."
"What if other people don't think so," Lee sat down to eat.
"Then that's them. You keep trying until someone thinks you are."

Lisa sat down; Lee said grace and then they ate.

"You should do something on your mom." Lisa said fixing plates.
"I really didn't know her," Lee said putting food in her mouth.
"Then what will you write on?"
"I thought on Kelly."
"Ok," Lisa took a drink of her juice.
"In her memory."
"I think she would like that," Lisa looked at Lee, *Will you be able to handle it?"*
"I think so."
"Well I'm here for you."
"I know, thanks."
"Don't mention it."
"No, I mean for everything. I don't think I would have made it without you and my sister."
"We're here for you."

Lisa kissed Lee.

Later that night, Lee sat in the living room and looked at the contest paper. Tossing the idea around in her head. Lee finally decides to enter.

Sitting there, Lee began to write something down on paper. When she finished, Lee looked at what she wrote and smiled.

We come, we go
We pass through earth only once in a lifetime
While we journey on, we make the most of the time we
have
Good times and bad times
Heartaches and pain
Laughter and cheers
We only have to give.
Friendship and love
Hope and preserver
These are the things I miss
From my friend I loved so dear.
Keep me in your heart
As I keep you in mines
Holding on to memories
Of a friend I long to see just once more
Even though my heart hurts from the day
You left me alone
I must maintain, I must be strong
Cause even after death, our friendship I hold on
We come, we go
We pass through earth only once in a lifetime
Your time as come and went
I miss you my friend, my sister
Until we meet again.

Lee reread the words, each time feeling something different. Feeling this was the one, she waited until Lisa and Renee read it before sending it in.

"That's beautiful." Renee said.
"Is this the one you're going to send in?" Lisa asked.
"Yep," unsure, *"unless you think I shouldn't..."*
"Baby, its fine." Lisa smiled at her, as Renee shook her head.

It was Sunday afternoon and Lee and Lisa were having Sunday dinner with Renee and Simon. Lee had just read the poem she entered into the writing contest.

"Are you always this critical of yourself?" Renee asked as she passed the food around to others.
"Yes." Lisa answered.
"Sometimes," Lee looked at Lisa.
"All the time," Lisa laughed.

Lisa, looked at Lee, laughed as she rubbed her shoulders and said *"Awe baby."*

Lee blushed.

"Why?" Renee asked in between bites.
"I never thought I was good enough or if people would like me," Lee dropped her head.
"Sis, I'm going to tell you something mom use to tell me as a child; "If you don't believe in you, then no one will."
"But"
"No buts. You'll do fine with that piece. It captures your friendship with Kelly and the love and respect you had for her."
"Baby, its good, just enter it."

Finally Lee reluctantly agreed. Renee got up and went over to the desk drawer and pulled out notebooks and handed it to Lee. Lee opened it up and inside was different short stories and poems on different subjects.

"Mom used to write, she loved it. She took time out after she got sick but started back up until she couldn't do it no more. You can keep it and go through it. Look at the many styles mom used. Hopefully one will help you."

Later that night, Lee looked through the notebook and read some of her mom's work. She was amazed at the talent her mom had, wishing she had that same gift. Reading her mom words, Lee began to feel a connection with her mom, feeling her presence, hearing as she speaks.

Beautiful child
Sleep tonight
Your day is done and night had come
The angels above watches over you
Protecting you as you lie in peace
Dream of good things, of hope and love
Until the day of light shines and your day begin a new
For I'm with you always
My beautiful child of mines.

My love
My heart belongs to thee
Even though you belong to someone else
How it yearns for your touch
The sweet words of your simple love
Longing for your smile
That lets me know things will be ok
Longing to look into your eyes
That lets me know how deep our love flows.

My Friend

Sometimes I sat and wonder how life plays it silly games
Bringing u into my world just to up and pull you away
Now I'm sitting here wishing
Things could go back to how things between us use to be

Never in my wildest dream did I think we would change
Thought we always be together, best friends until the
end,
Never did I think u would not be here for me
Forever and forever, that how it should been.

My friend, my friend
How I miss calling your name,
The one true thing in my life
Now I'll never be the same…
My friend, my friend
How I miss the time we shared,
How I wish you were here, because things aren't the
same.

Death is coming
It knocks on my door
I'm not afraid of it
Because I know my Lord is with me
I'm walking through it with open arms
Not scare or running away
My God had kept me
With his loving and saving grace
My time is winding down
No need for tears or sad goodbyes

Walking with me is my Lord and Savior
I have no fears for with his blood
My soul is free.

Months passed and Lee continued to work hard in school. She maintained a B average in her classes. One of her instructors offers her encouragement.

"You should make a collection of your thoughts," she said. *"I think other people might like to read them."*
"That's sound like a good idea." Lisa said.

Lee was helping Lisa put grocery away. Afterwards, Lee and Lisa went into the living room to watch TV.

"You have so much inside of you, putting your thoughts into words, exactly helps. You have so much to offer people."
"My thoughts are personal though," Lee said.
"Lee, you have something special. Not many people can sit down and write like you do."
"I never saw it that way."
"Baby, you open up when you write. You let people know how you feel inside."

Lee sat quietly, pondering what Lisa had said. She really never believed in herself enough to see the positive side.

"You should give it a try, you owe yourself that much."

Taking Lisa advice, Lee started keeping a journal of everything she felt. With help from her instructor, Lee organized her thoughts into book form. She now had in written form, her personal thoughts and feelings.

Lee shared with Lisa what she had written. Lisa was impressed. She told Lee how proud she was and to keep it up.

"Don't stop," Lisa said.

Everyday Lee wrote something different in her journal. The title; *All about Lee: My Thoughts and Feelings from Inside.*

Lee wrote on many subjects; her father and how his death affected her, her sister, the void of losing her mom before she got to know her. Lisa, Kelly but mostly on her being gay and what all the entails and mean to her as a black woman.

Lee never really knew she had this much feelings locked up inside of her. The more she wrote the more she learned about who she was as a person, not black or gay. Years of being afraid of what others had to say or think about her started flowing out like the Mississippi River after the ice melts. Pressure from the weight of the world slowly lifted off her shoulders as Lee was realizing who she was. She could be and do anything she wanted once she put her mind to it.

"See, told you, just be you. Don't let what other people said decide who you gonna be in life. Your happiness should be all that matters, not someone else's." Kelly's voice played in Lee's head.

Lee also realized through her journals that regardless of your current circumstance, that you can be better. To not give up and to keep trying until you get it right.

Chapter Twenty-Four

It was Monday afternoon. Lee had received a certified letter in the mail. It was from the writing contest committee. Lee opened the letter, her face lit up after only reading a few lines. Lee ran back into the house and to the bedroom.

Lisa was making the bed when Lee burst through the doorway.

"Babe, babe," she ran in.

Lisa looked startled as Lee couldn't contain her excitement and handed Lisa the letter. Lisa sat down on the edge of the bed and read it. Lisa looked up and smiled at Lee.

"It said your poem came in fifth."

Lee beamed with pride.

"I'm surprise it came in fifth, I thought maybe eleventh or fifteen or something," she said.
"It's still good. See I told you, you had something special inside you, and all you had to do was believe. I'm so proud of you."

Lisa stood up and hugged Lee.

"You're going to call Renee and share this with her?"
"No, I'm going to wait until tomorrow when I get off work. I'll go over to her house and show her."
"Baby, I'm really am proud of you. After going through so much, you're doing so well."

Tuesday afternoon. Lee was at work. She was working fast so she can get off early and go by Renee house. She couldn't wait to tell her the good news.

Around noon, Lee boss came over to her.

"Lee, phone call!"

She went to his office and took the call.

"Hello...."
"Lee..."

Lisa was on the other end.

"Hey. What's up?" Lee said.
"Lee, baby, you need to leave work, it's your sister...,
Renee...she..."

Lee listened as Lisa told her that Renee was in the hospital and it didn't look good. After hanging up with Lisa, a sick feeling overcame her. Lee quickly told her boss what had happen and left for the hospital.

At the hospital, Lee headed to the eight floor nurses station where she tried to find out about Renee.

"I was told my sister was brought here."
"May I have her name please?"
"Renee Wilson."

The lady at the desk checked her computer. Finding the information, she looked at Lee.

"If you can have a seat the doctor will be with you
shortly."

"Can you please tell me what's wrong with my sister?"
"The doctor will have to do that miss. I'm sorry."

Lee went and took a seat. She took a deep breath and sighed looking up at the ceiling. A few seconds later, Lisa came down the hall.

"Lee! Lee!"
"What happen?"
Lee got up and went over to Lisa.
"Renee passed out at the house and was unresponsive. When the squad came, she had no heart beat or pulse."

Lee looked at Lisa afraid of what's next.

"Baby, Renee flat line twice, once at the house and then again en route here."
"Who found her?"
"Simon. He called your aunt then 911."
"Is she dea…" unable to finish.
"No, there working on her now. Your aunt is with the doctors."

Lisa took Lee back to where Aunt Fannie was. Aunt Fannie was talking to one of the doctors as Simon and Keisha were in the waiting area. Aunt Fannie looked up and saw Lee and Lisa.

"Doctor Smith, this is my other niece, Lee, this is Renee younger sister."
"How do you do," he shook her hand.
"As I was explaining to your aunt, right now Ms. Wilson is stable."
"What happen?" Lee asked.
"Ms. Wilson had an aneurysm."
"A what?" Lee looked around for the answer.

"Aneurysm, it's where a blood vessels erupts causing bleeding in the brain. We were able to go in and stop the bleeding but there was swelling to the brain though."

"Is my sister going to be ok?" Lee trying to stay composed.

"At this moment, we don't know. Ms. Wilson suffered some damages to her left side of her brain and we don't know the extent of it. Her blood pressure was real low when she came in and here. Vitals were unstable. Right now, we are monitoring her for a possible stroke."

Lee stumbled back against the wall not believing what she was hearing. This can't be happening she mumbled to herself. Lee felt like her whole world was crashing in around her.

Lee struggled to find her words, careful not to betray the one feeling she had deep inside.

"Is my sister going to die?"

"Like I said I don't have an answer to that. The first twenty-four hours are critical. We have to wait and see."

"Thank you Doctor Smith for everything," Aunt Fannie said, shaking his hand.

Lisa held Lee hand and told her everything will be alright as they go and take a seat. Lee struggled to understand why this had happened to Renee. Aunt Fannie came and sat down next to her.

"It's in the good Lord hands now," she said as she patted Lee's leg. *"Renee is a fighter, she'll pull through."*

Lee looked at her aunt and saw her differently. Instead of a person who always judging someone, preaching(bible thumping), and thought someone should live according to the

bible. Someone who was stern and set in their ways. Aunt
Fannie was showing a side of compassion and sympathy. She
allowed herself to show a little weakness and vulnerability.
Aunt Fannie tried to be strong but in her eyes, Lee saw fear and
concern.

"Auntie, what happen?" Lee asked.
*"Well child, I was on the phone with Renee and she was
telling me she was having a real bad headache. I told her to
take some Advil and go rest and call me later. The next thing I
knew, Simon called me and said that Renee wouldn't wake up. I
told him to call 911. When they got there, they couldn't revive
her."*

Lee looked at her aunt.

"You said she complain of a bad headache?"
*"Yes, I knew at the Thanksgiving dinner something
wasn't right. She complained of pain the night you were in the
ER."*

Lee looked at Lisa who's in shock. Lee felt bad as they
both knew why.

"You didn't know."
"Didn't know what?" Aunt Fannie looked at Lee then
Lisa.

Lee explained to her aunt about the episode Renee had
when she was at her house.

*"Honey, don't go blaming yourself. If Renee made you
promise not to tell me, then you did the right. Surely she had
her reason."*

Aunt Fannie looked down the hall.

"All we can do now is pray," Aunt Fannie sighed.

After a while Renee doctor let Lee go in to see her. When Lee entered the room, she was unprepared for what she saw.

The room was a mess. Blood was everywhere. Papers and supplies are scattered throughout the room from where the doctors worked to save Renee life.

Renee was lying in bed, her eyes tape shut. She was hooked up to different machines and had tubes coming out from different areas. She had one tube going to her neck, one connected to her head and groin area and a catchier in her arm.

Renee was hooked up to a monitor that showed her vitals.

She had a tube coming out of her mouth and was connected to a big oxygen machine next to the bed. It helped Renee with her breathing. She laid in a coma. Lee watched as Renee chest rise and fell as the machine pumped oxygen into her lungs.

She had two IV coming from her arms. One for medicine and sodium chloride and the other for blood.

Renee looked fragile and helpless. Her head swollen twice the normal size.

Lee walked over to her sister. Tears streamed down her face. She held Renee hands, and their cold.

Lisa and Aunt Fannie come in. Lisa walked over to Lee and put her arm around her.

"Baby," she whispered. *"She's going to be ok,"* Lisa tried to have some hope.

Lee felt helpless, unable to do anything for her sister as tears continues to fall.

"I need some air," Lee said shaking her head.

Lee quickly walked out the room.

"Wait," Lisa said hurrying behind her.

Lisa turned to go but Aunt Fannie stopped her.

"Let her be," Aunt Fannie said to Lisa. *"Sometimes it's best to let someone deal with what's bothering them alone."*

Lisa stood at the door and looked out as Lee walked down the hallway. She knew Aunt Fannie was right but it's hard to stand back and watch Lee hurt and go through pain all over again.

Aunt Fannie looked back at Renee.

"Lord, please help them both through this."

Chapter Twenty-Five

Lee was sitting in the Chaplin room. She was trying to make sense of everything that had happen today. Lee never imagined seeing her sister like this. As tears fell down her face, Lee softly prayed.

"Lord, please don't take my sister from me, she's all I got. I lost my mom, my father and my best friend. Please help her."

Lee remembered what her father used to say; *"Always know, no matter what, you are never alone. Someone is always looking out for you."* She remembers the promise to Kelly and the words her sister would said to her; *"I'm always here for you when you need me."* Suddenly, Lee felt alone and scared.

As Lee sat, Lisa came in. She walked to where she sitting and sat down next to her. Lisa held her as Lee cried in her arms.

"I can't lose someone else." Lee cried.
"You won't, everything will be alright."

Lee sat up and wiped her eyes.

"I know in the beginning I was scared about meeting Renee but now…"

Suddenly Lee laughed.

"What's funny," Lisa startled.
"I was thinking about my father."
"What about?"

"I knew the woman he was married to wasn't my real mom, he told me."

"I didn't know that," Lisa was amazed.

"He told me when I was old enough to understand, about ten, me and him sat down one day and really talked about it."

"So."

"He told me my mom was a beautiful and smart woman who had a sense of humor. She was always doing some practical joke on him. I can't remember, but apparently she did something to him one day and he didn't speak to her for weeks."

"So they knew each other?" Lisa was shocked.

"Yes, from college, they were best friends. He said at first she told him she wasn't going tell him about me, but when she got sick, she felt he had the right to know."

"Wow!" Lisa exclaimed. "But I thought you didn't know that your mom was dying?"

"I didn't, not until Mrs. Carlton told us. He only told me she was sick but never anything else. I guess he felt I couldn't handle that part at a young age."

"Like your sister."

"I suppose."

Lisa didn't said anything instead just looked at Lee.

"I asked my father if he loved my mom," Lee said serious tone.

"What he said?"

"He told me he did, that she was his best friend. He said, "I cared deeply about my wife but at that time we were going through a rough marriage. He went to my mother and being good friends with her, he felt he could talk to her."

"She listened to me, she didn't judge. You mother knew I was having problems in my marriage but she also knew I would never leave my wife. She told me, "We've been friends

for too long and we never lied to each other and I won't start
now. If you're not happy with her then leave but only if you had
done all you can as a husband to make things work. Bottom
line, you have to be happy and true to what you want."

"Your mom sound like she really cared about your
father," Lisa amazed at what she hears.

"She did and he cared for her the same way."

"So how did you come about?"

"My father found comfort in her. She made him smile
and laugh. She bought the best out of him. But they both
understood nothing could come out of it. When my mother
finally told him about me, he told me she said; "I have no
regrets, none. I love you."

"That's deep." Lisa admitted.

A few minutes later Simon came into the room.

"Aunt Lee, auntie said the doctor wants to see the
family."

Lee looked at Lisa, took a deep breath and got up.
Placing her hand on her nephew shoulders, Lee, Lisa and Simon
walked out.

Chapter Twenty-Six

Everybody was gathered outside of Renee room; Lee, Lisa, Aunt Fannie, Keisha and Simon. Doctor Smith wants to discuss Renee condition with them.

"As you all know, Renee had suffered some damaged to her left side of her brain caused by the aneurysm. We however don't know the extent of the damage until the swelling went down. We have her stabilize and are monitoring her for changes. Right now, she is in a induce coma so her body can heal."

Doctor Smith paused to give the family time to take in what he had said before going on.

"In case she took a complete turn for the worse, I would like to know how you would like us to proceed."
"I don't understand?" Aunt Fannie replied.
"In case Ms. Wilson doesn't respond, would you like for us to disconnect her from life support?"

Everyone looked at each other not knowing what to say. Finally Aunt Fannie spoke.

"I raised Renee every since my sister passed away. I promise my sister that I would do everything in my being to keep her safe and to love her. I did that. I can said as head of the family, we will wait to see what happens and ask that you do all you can to help her until you can't help her no more, and I'll pray to God to save her."
"As you wish and I promise to do everything we can for her."
"Thank you."

Aunt Fannie went into the room and sat at Renee bedside. Lee follows behind with Lisa, Keisha and Simon.

Simon stood at the head of the bed and whispered *"I love you mommy,"* as he strokes her hair. Lee and Lisa stood at the foot of the bed, Keisha behind her mom.

Aunt Fannie looked old and tired. Her eyes red from crying, her shoulders droops as if the weight of the world sat on them, her face long from worrying.

Aunt Fannie grabbed Renee hands and looked at the monitor.

Beep...beep...beep...beep.

Heart beat.

Whoosh...swish tap...whoosh...swish tap...

Life support machine.

A nurse came in and gave Renee medicine through her IV line and checks her vitals.
"She stable," she said to Aunt Fannie writing in the chart, *"is there anything I can get for you,"* looked at the family.
"No thank you," Aunt Fannie said, Lee and Lisa nod no, *"your kindness is greatly appreciated."*
"If you need anything, push the call button."

After Aunt Fannie said ok, the nurse left the room.

"Baby," Lee said rubbing Renee hands, *"The doctor are doing all they can for you. Now it's up to you and God."*

Aunt Fannie bows her head.

"Lord, let thy will be done."
"A-men," everyone said.

Days turned into weeks and Lee had been at the hospital everyday. She talks to Mrs. Carlton and her boss who both said that is where she should be.

"Take your time, come back when your ready," her boss told her.
"Your family is in my prayers," Mrs. Carlton said.

Lee calls Alexis and told her.

"Call me if you need anything. Mom and Kim said that they will be praying for your sister too."

Weeks turned into months. Lee and her aunt rotate out so the other can get some rest. Sometimes Lisa would stay all night for support to Lee when she spend the night.

Other times Lee would go by herself. At times she would read to Renee what she wrote or just talk to her. Often Lee would just sat and hope and pray Renee would wake up and be alright.

"Lord, please don't let my sister die."

It had been three months since Renee been hospitalize and her condition hadn't change. Her vitals are stable but she was still in a coma. Every day the family hopes for some good news.

A few more weeks passed and the doctors said there was still no responds from Renee. Even though she was stable, the doctors still said Renee was not out of the woods yet. Things could still go either way and Renee had yet to open her eyes.

"Statically, people who suffered brain aneurysm don't survive the first twenty-four hours. Even though she still here, there are some side effects from it, like; speech impediment, coordination, or permanent disability. We just have to wait and see if she wakes up."

Aunt Fannie and Lee had been at Renee side no stop, hoping and praying for a miracle. It also during this time that Lee and her aunt get to know each other better.

"Renee, we need you to open your eyes so you can come home. Your son needs you, well all need you. Come on baby, open your eyes for auntie."

Aunt Fannie speaks to Renee rubbing her arm; Lee stood near the window looked on.

"Lee," she motions for her to sat next to her, *"there something I want to talk to you about."*
"Ok."
"I want to clear up any misconceptions that you may have about me or vise versa."
Lee begins to have that uneasy feeling not knowing where this was leading.

"I know you think that I don't particular care for you."
"I do." Lee stated.
"Well that's not true, I do."
"Ok."
"And I want to apologize if you feel that way."
"It just seems that you think you're better than me because I'm…"
"Gay," she finished.
"Well, yeah." Lee got up.

"Again, I'm sorry you felt that way."

"It just seems like that especially after our first meeting in the ER."

"Well, maybe I came off rough that night. Now don't get me wrong, I do believe in what the Bible said about homosexuality, that it is a sin against God."

"But," Lee interjected.

"But let me finish," Aunt Fannie stops her, *"look, we all have to live our on lives and were not perfect, the Bible said so. Now I will admit that I do go sprouting off scriptures from the Bible, that's me. However I do know that Jesus also talked about judging, forgiveness, and love. Now do I agree with your lifestyle, no I don't, and I'm sorry if that bothers you. I be lying to you if I said I did but you're my niece, and were family, and I do love you and worry about you. I know you had a hard life and this is all new to you but if you give me a chance, I would like to know you,"* pointed to Lee.

"I want you to understand though, this is me."

"As long as you understand this is how I feel on this subject."

"I understand."

"Look, I can't judge you, like I said, we all error in our ways. I'm not perfect, I had an affair on my husband but God forgave me. But you're right though, in the end, the only person you have to answer to is God. He's the only one who can judge me or you."

Aunt Fannie got up and hugged Lee.

"I do love you."
"I love you too."
"Forgive me"
"Yeah."
Turned and looked at Renee, *"Now it's up to you."*

Lee stood there wishing for the same thing.

It was raining outside this morning and Lee had just relieved her aunt so she can go home and get some rest before coming back this afternoon. Lisa told Lee she would be up after work.

Lee put her hands inside her jacket pockets and filled a piece of paper. Pulling it out, she realized it was the letter from the writing contest.

"I wanted to share this with you," Lee said speaking about the letter, *"but I'll wait till you get better."*

Lee opened the folded paper that's had the poem on it and began to read it aloud.

"You said you like it." Lee said folding it back up and putting it back inside her jacket pocket. *"You got to get better. We have so much to get caught up on. I need my sister. I can't lose another person I love. Fight Renee! Please fight, open your eyes!"*

Something catches Lee eyes. She looked down and thinks she seen something but thinks her eyes or playing tricks.

"My eyes must be tired," Lee said to herself, rubbing them.

Lee looked at the blanket and there was slight movement again. Looking closely, Lee saw movement near Renee fingertip. Now the blanket began to move around the feet and hands. Lee looked at her sister, her heart beating faster, hands becoming sweaty.

"Sis," Lee looked at Renee.

Lee got up, *"Sis, can you hear me?"* She asked becoming excited.

"Um-hum," Lee hears.

Looking at Renee, Lee saw her sister head slightly move from side to side.

"Renee if you can hear me, open your eyes." Lee pleaded.

"Um- hum," Renee moaned.

"Come on, you can do it, just open you eyes."

Renee slowly opened her eyes.

"Sis!"

Lee ran to the door and threw it open.

"Doctor, I need a doctor," Lee yells.

Lee went back into the room and to Renee bedside. Renee looked around and then looked at Lee.

"Oh sis," Lee cried.

Lee leaned down and hugged her sister. Soon Doctor Smith and his nurse come into the room followed by Aunt Fannie, Lisa, Keisha, Simon and Cortez. Everybody looked as Lee stepped back.

"Mommy!" Simon yell.

"Thank you Jesus," Aunt Fannie throwing her hands in the air and rejoices as Keisha cried.

Lisa put her arm around Lee's waist and smiled as tears fell. Lee was happy and thankful.

Doctor Smith checks Renee vitals: normal, then gave her voice commands to follow:

"Squeeze my fingers."
"Squeeze my hands."
"Follow the pen light with your eyes."

She was able to do it all.

Doctor Smith turned and looked at the family.

"I said Ms. Wilson is on the road to recovery," he said smiling.
"Thank you God, the storm had finally passed over," she shouts.

Lee looked out the window and smiled to herself. Yes it had. Lee turned around and looked at her sister who gave her a weak smile. Going over to the bed, Lee joined in on the celebration with her family; talking, laughing, crying and many thanks to God for bringing Renee through.

Chapter Twenty-Seven

It's been almost three months since Renee had her aneurysm. With hard work from physical therapy and support from her family, Renee made a full recovery.

"So what are you ladies doing for Easter?"

Aunt Fannie looked at Lee and Lisa and asked. Looking at each other, Lee said nothing.

Lee and Lisa were at Renee house fixing Easter baskets. Aunt Fannie is boiling the eggs; Lee and Lisa are putting the baskets together while Simon and Cortez are decorating the eggs.

Renee came into the kitchen with help from Keisha. She walked with a noticeable limp and had to use a cane. She sat down, looked around and smiled. She never thought she would live to see this day. Simon ran over to his mom and hugged her and softly whisper *I love you mommy.*

"I love you too baby," kissed him on the check.
"As I was saiding, why don't you two come to church with us tomorrow?" Aunt Fannie said.
"I don't know, it's been awhile since I been. Plus me and Lisa…"
Aunt Fannie waves them off, *"no excuses."*
"I don't have anything to wear," Lee tried to interject.
"I don't want to hear that, it's settled, tomorrow morning at New Zion, eleven sharp."

Lee looked at Lisa and then Renee not knowing what to said.

"If I was you two, I said yes mam`e," Lisa laughed.

Lee and Lisa both said yes mam`e as everybody snickers.

"Besides," Aunt Fannie smiled, *"I'm going to tell you the same thing someone smart told me; only God can judge someone."*

Aunt Fannie looked at Renee who nodded in agreement then looked at Lee who smiled back.

Chapter Twenty-Eight

Easter morning and Lee, Renee, Lisa, Aunt Fannie along with their sons and her cousin are at church.

The service was nice and Lee felt welcome as she sat and listen to the choir sing *How I Got Over* and *Hallelujah Any How*. When the minister asked if there are any first time visitors, Lee was hesitant to get up, but with some coxing, both Lee and Lisa stood as other members come by and welcome them and invite them back.

Lee listened to her aunt sing a solo and listened to the minster preach on forgiveness, hope, faith and God love.

"For God so love the world, that he gave his only begotten son that whosoever believes in him shall not perish but have everlasting life."
"This is what God love is all about, he loves us in spite of who we are. Regardless of what you think about yourself know that God loves you today and wants to share his love with you.

He also preaches on the power of prayer and it working for those who have faith.

"When you go to God, believe that what you ask for he will provide. Stand on his word, he won't let you down."

He talks about family and values and instruct those to love one another had the Lord love them.

"The Lord said to love one another had I have love you."

"Speaking of prayer, I see today that Sis. Renee is here with us. As some of you know, Sis. Renee a few months ago was in the hospital due to an aneurysm. The doctors said that she might not make it, that it look bad, but I'm here to tell you that God is in the healing business, when they said we can't, he said, but I can. Church, there is nothing to hard for my God to handle."

A-men can be heard throughout the church.

"I'm also happy to welcome Sis. Renee sister Lee and her friend who are here today for service. Aunt Fannie had informed me, that Sis. Renee and her sister had been separated after their mom passed away and after all these years, the sisters were finally reunited. Wasn't God good, don't we serve an all powerful God, a God who can take something bad and turn it into something good."

A-men again come from the congregation. People were on their feet clapping. Some coming over to give them a hug. Lee looked slightly embarrass at the attention she was receiving. She looked at her sister who smiled at her.

"To Lee, your aunt told me you were nervous about coming today. I'm here to tell you, it doesn't matter who you are or what you do, the Lord still loves you. You are his child."

Lisa pat Lee on the leg as Lee wiped back a tear. She felt love, not love that came from a love one or spouse but of an unconditional love.

"Before we conclude today service, Aunt Fannie had a special treat for us. As she came forward, let's show her our love."

Aunt Fannie stood and walked toward the microphone. She grabbed it and spoke.

"I'm thankful for your prayers and well wishes for my family in our time of need and I'm also thankful to have them here today. These last few months have brought us closer together. I have been taught that no matter what you do in life, we are all the same and that God love us the same."

"A-men!"

"I would like my niece Lee to come up here and join me. I learned that like my sister, she too likes to sing."

Lee looked at Renee, she know that her and her aunt planned this. Renee looked at her and told her to go on up. Lee looked at Lisa who encourages her also.

"Let's help my niece on," Aunt Fannie began clapping.

Everyone claps and encourages her. Lee finally got up and walked to the front of the church. When she reaches the front, her aunt hugged her.

"I love you," Aunt Fannie whispered.

Lee looked out and saw her family happy and smiling at her. Cortez gave her a thumps up. Lee turned and looked at her aunt who reaches out and held her hand.

"When Renee was in the hospital, Lee was there everyday by her sister side. One day as she was sitting there by the bedside, I came in and stood near the door. Lee didn't know I was there. As I stood there listening, Lee was singing this song as Renee laid there in bed. I would like to sing that same song with her today."

The organist starts to play. Lee recognizes the song and
begins to smile, *It's Ok* by Bebe and Cece Winans. She began
to sing;

> *Maybe we can talk it over*
> *And save our hopes and dreams*
> *Though the waves seem endless*
> *Somehow we'll cross this angry sea*
> *With love all things are possible*
> *If we just believe*

Aunt Fannie joined in;

> *I need to know, (Aunt) yes it ok*
> *Can I hurdle this storm, (Aunt) yes but only together*
> *With love in our hearts, (Aunt) the only way*
> *Somehow, things will work out just you wait and see*

As Lee and her aunt sing, Lee felt a rush of peace came.
She believes in the words she is singing.

Aunt Fannie sings;

> *See real life confrontations*
> *Cause our vows to break*
> *But I learned the word forgiveness*
> *Can time chade the pain away*
> *True love made our hearts inseparable*
> *If we just believe*

> *I need to know, (Lee) yes it's okay*
> *Can I hurdle this storm, (Lee) yes but only together*
> *With God in our hearts, (Lee) the only way*
> *Somehow, things will work out just you*
> *Wait and see*

Lee and Aunt Fannie together;

But right now it hurts so bad
And felt so bad
But tomorrow waits with laughter
If we endure the tears then joy came after

Looking out into the congregation, she saw Renee swaying back in forth. Lee felt thankful for her sister. Lee was worried that her sister wouldn't accept her, but she did. She didn't think she would have another chance with her, afraid her sister would die. But she kept hope and God heard and answered her prayer.

Looked at her aunt;

I need to know, (Aunt) you need to know
It's gonna be okay
Can I hurdle this storm, (Aunt) only together
With love in our hearts, (Aunt) the only way
And somehow, somehow i can feel love again
Somehow, things have worked out
Cause you stayed with me
(Aunt)I'm glad to know it's okay, it's okay.

The congregations stood on their feet and gave a thunderous applauds. Lee hugged her aunt then looked out. Renee was standing and clapping and waving her hands back and forth. She saw Lisa clapping and shouting. Cortez smiling yells yeah as Simon hugged his mom and clapped along with Keisha.

Lee hugged her aunt again, and left the choir stand and went back to her seat. Renee gave her a hug and told her how proud she was.

"I love you sis, I'm so proud of you."

"I love you too."

After church, Lee and her family gathered at Renee house for Easter dinner. As Lee sat, she looked around the table at each person.

To Renee: showed her loved and never judged her for who she was.

To Lisa: been her friend through it all. Taught her to accept herself for who she is.

Her aunt: taught her that no matter what the problem is, God is in control.

Simon, Cortez and her cousin: no matter what, we will always be family.

Lee thought about those who have passed on before her.

Her mom, even though she never got to see her daughter grow up, Lee knew she loved her.

Her father, loved his little girl and made it possible that she never be alone after he passed.

Kelly, taught her to live her life and no one else's and to always be herself.

To friends and teachers: Do all you can before you give up. Be everything in life you can be and to don't settle for anything less and always try. Life owes you nothing. You have to be willing to go out and get what you want and learn that to every action is a reaction. Be willing to accept consequence for whatever you do.

Finally Lee thinks upon herself. She realized that throughout all she'd been through, the ups and downs, she had never been alone. That people who loved her most had always had her back. She learned that it was ok to open up and not shut people out. They only want to help and what was best for me. They also understood enough to let you figure things out on your own. And most important, that we are all humans and not perfect that we fall and make mistook. See the good in you instead of the bad all the time, learn to love you first and be happy with who you are on the inside and not worried about what someone else things of you.

Lee got that second chance like Kelly told her. She had a sister who loved and cared for her. Who only wanted her to be happy. Lee and Renee were a family now and Lee finally had closure in a chapter of her life.

EPILOGUE

In conclusion, I learned to believe in myself and love and accept me for who I am. I also had to learn that everybody wasn't going to like or accept me and that was cool. That changing me for someone else was not going to make it any better. That in the end they still might not like me. That's life. Even though this story is fictional, the characters are based upon real people in my life who taught me and influence me throughout my life. Those who stood by my side when things got rough and others bailed on me and believed in me when I didn't believe in myself. I would like to say thank you for your support and determination in helping me to get to the next level.

It's been eighteen years since I was gay, and only a few years ago since I decided to leave that life.

It's been a struggle and at times I didn't think I was going to make it. Sliding back into a life that once ago I created for me. But with help from a supporting cast and determination to make it this time and believing if I just only trust and lean on God, that I could and would make it. I only hope that these words will encourage and help someone who is struggling in life or going through some hard times. Know you're not alone. That there is someone always looking out for you.

I know some people might not like what I wrote or can't accept it, but one thing I come to believe is true; *Only God Can Judge Me and He Is My Judge.*

Thank you and may God bless you.

www.ingramcontent.com/pod-product-compliance
Lightning Source LLC
Chambersburg PA
CBHW021103130626
46554CB00002B/514